## Coming Home Logan's Wish

Copyright 2013 Adeline Moore
Coming Home Series Book One

Paperback Book published in Canada
ISBN:9780991959358

Cover Art by A.R.M
Inset courtesy of free digital photos.net

~~Dedication~~
If you believe something will happen in your life then it will.

# Table of Contents

## ~~ Coming Home ~ Logan's Wish

Logan heaved a sigh of weary relief, almost home. He had been counting the minutes for the last twenty miles. It had been a long six weeks, this time trucking horses from one side of canada to the other and just to make things interesting the odd haul to and from the United States,thanks to dad.

His Dad was the perpetual optimist saying its only gonna add an extra day when in fact he was lucky if it wasn't a week or more. Well he was home now back on his turf, the Wild Horse ranch had been in his family for generations, four hundred years of Mcleans had owned the forty thousand acres of prime foothills land he and Dillon were running now.

Pulling in the gateway, under the Wild Horse sign he smiled, great to be here he thought time to catch up on all he had missed over a brew with his brother. Logan was the wheels and Dillon was the brains making the ranch the most successful horse breeding operation in Alberta.

Coming to a stop in front of the house he shared with his brother he shut his transport off, opened his door and climbed down. Half way across the concrete parking pad, the front door opened and Dillon stepped out onto the porch.

"Hey Logan, you made it."

"Ya its been a long time, I'm looking forward to my own bed. You have any beer?"

"All kinds, come on in."Dillon said smirking.

"Been looking forward to a cold one since Red Deer. Its been a long ass haul this time. Hope you don't have any more lined up for awhile?"

"Two months till the next one and that's only to Dad's in Montana." Logan nodded and followed Dillon into the house, through the cavernous living room to the kitchen where Logan found his chair waiting for him at the table. Dillon handed him the beer he had been dreaming about, sitting down across from him waiting till he finished his first swallow. "What's new around here?" Logan asked.

"Hmm well we have ten new foals, all fine. Added two new hands to help out and we have a resident biologist camping out at the green spring.What's new with you?"

Dillon asked with a satisfied grin on his face.

"Nothing just hauling. Still having the dreams so nothing has changed for me there.What is this biologist studying up there?"

"The wolf population is all I know Amiela says research is the only way to know more about them.Seems pretty important to her anyway."

"I suppose it is. Is this research impacting operations?

Logan wondered how many problems they were about to encounter.

"It is, making things easier, we know where the pack is and we turn out in different sectors away from them, so that should lessen the loss ratio considerably."

"Better bottom line then, that's acceptable. So when do I get to meet this woman you seem so fond of?"

"Well I have invited her for dinner tomorrow night to discuss the project to date."

"Great gives me time to get some rest.What's for dinner?"

"Pot roast. Thing is Amiela keeps our relationship strictly business no matter which way I approach her to move matters to a personal level.I'm thinking she's not interested in me then I catch a look or an expression and I know she is. What do you think I should do?"

"Off hand I think maybe she's shy or inhibited in some way."Logan glanced to his brother for feedback holding his bottle up for a refill. He thought for a moment how to best answer Logan's question then he replied.

"She doesn't seem to be its more like something is holding her back."Dillon explained going to the fridge for a couple more beers.

"Perhaps its not the time for her to get involved with anyone given her work."

"Well if thirty three is too soon then when!"Dillon replied exasperated by the subject.

"I'm going to speculate here but just maybe she is looking for a non-traditional type of relationship."

"Could be, lets see what happens when she comes for dinner then."

Not much can be done right now anyway Logan thought before asking."You mentioned you hired a couple new guys?

"Ya its going to be a great year, busier then ever so I thought it was time to up the manpower around here. With any luck they will be here as long as everyone else."

"People do tend to be carried off our place,been that way a long long time."

"How is dad doing?"

"He is happy down there with Jesse, smart move for him to buy that ranch and move, now he has her and his life is making sense again."

Logan wished fervently in that moment that his was doing so well. "It was hard on him after mom died being here without her.So many memories of them exist here."

"He's come to terms with it now, says he's living again and by the looks of it he is.Those two are like a couple of kids sometimes, its nice to see him happy."

"I think when you take the load of horses down to him I will come along, have a visit."Dillon liked the idea of getting away for awhile seeing something new maybe meet someone new. Nothing was happening for him here at the moment.

"Good idea. Now its time for me to get some sleep. Goodnight Dillon."

Dillon tidied up the kitchen, grabbed a scotch and went out on the veranda taking in the night reflecting on the conversation he and Logan had over dinner.

The sun was lighting the sky as Logan awoke anxious to start a new day.Rising from his large bed he padded to the bathroom naked,turning on the shower he adjusted the temperature to cool hoping his erection would soften. The dream of the blond, blue eyed vixen with all those luscious curves had come again making him rise to the occasion. He had been having the same dream for two years.It started after his last relationship failed miserably. He knew the starlet in his dreams was the one but as yet he still had to meet.'I need to get laid.' He thought but knew it probably wasn't happening today and tonight he had the dinner with Dillon and Amiela. Possible candidate but not very likely,if she wasn't swayed by his blond haired blue eyed brother then it was unlikely she would be turned on by his dark brooding mug.His mother had always told him he was just like his dad and he agreed in looks yes, demeanor no, he was much more controlling than his father, harder in most ways, whereas Dillon looked just like their mother, had her commanding personality but preferred to reason rather than dictate.

Logan soaped up finding the cool water refreshing 'not doing much for my woody though' rinsing he turned the water to cold letting it run down his front finally his cock softened.

Turning off the water he exited grabbing a large fluffy towel he dried himself, brushed his teeth, shaved and brushed his short black hair.

Entering the bedroom he dove straight into his closet getting jeans,blue cotton t-shirt,underwear and dark blue socks.Sauntering into the kitchen a few minutes later he found Slim at the stove making breakfast.

"Hey what's cooking Slim?"Logan asked grabbing a cup, pouring himself a coffee.

"All your favorites,what else.Been a long time since you were here last, how's your dad doing?"

"He's good, happy, finally getting back into things. Of course Jesse has helped a lot."

"Nothing like a good woman to help a man through the rough times."

"Really so why are you single then?"

Logan had been wondering why he was still single.

"Told you I have never found the one."

"That I can relate too. Me either yet."

"You will one day soon I'm sure of that. Now sit, eat before everything gets cold."

Logan dug into the best ham,eggs,bacon and toast on the planet as far as he was concerned. Slim's raspberry jam was legend on the wildhorse, been Logan's favorite from the time he was little.
Dillon appeared looking worse for wear,looking up Logan scowled at him "Have a bad night?"
"I couldn't sleep for thinking about Amiela and wondering why she keeps side stepping away every time I make a move.  Fell asleep about four."
"Are you talking about the biologist up at green spring?" Slim asked smirking.
Dillon just shook his groggy head in the affirmative.
"Maybe she doesn't like blonds Dillon, not every woman is attracted to you, you know."
"Well gee thanks for the vote of confidence Slim!You just made my day."
"Well you can't have them all. One is more than enough if you ask me.
She's coming for dinner tonight why don't you just out and ask her? See you boys later I have work to do." With that Slim up and left Logan and Dillon staring at each other.
"Guess I better get the repairs done to the truck and trailer before I have to go again. See you later Dillon, stop stewing, I'm sure everything will come clear soon.

## ~~Coming Around~~

Amiela arrived back at her fifth wheel trailer at green spring around five.Well time for a shower and change of clothes before I have to leave for Dillon's place. He did say seven I hope.Checking her phone calendar yes it was, good I can catalog these samples before I leave.

TGIF she thought, its been a grueling five weeks, time for some fun.

Everything done,she stripped off her clothes on her way to the bathroom, turning on the shower she took her sports bra and panties off. Stepping inside the warm water started relieving the ache in her muscles from a tough day that started at four in the morning.

Field work was always like this but she loved it anyway.

Lathering with her favorite apple body wash she felt better. She washed her hair, rinsed and stepped out to a slight chill.Wrapping a towel around her petite body she secured it over her breasts, then wrapped her head in a smaller one turban style.

Looking through her closet she found a pair of red capris she matched with a white peasant blouse with red and gold embroidery around the neckline.She liked it because she could wear it on or off the shoulder and it always traveled well.

Finding her strappy red and gold beaded sandals she looked at the time, just enough to get dressed and leave.

Toweling her hair she brushed it out put on mascara and lip gloss leaving her hair to dry on the way over to the wild horse.

Finding her matching red lace thong panties and bra she slipped them on then her blouse and capris.Sandals on check, phone, purse got them.

Grabbing a light jacket and keys she locked up got in her truck and off she went. Driving along a tad over the speed limit she thought about the last time she came to give Dillon her progress report. It was lunch of which she enjoyed immensely.

If she wanted him given the signals he was putting out she could have him no problem. But back to her lifelong dilemma she Amiela Anderson wanted just a bit more than that. She was definitely attracted to him, just to bad he didn't have a brother she was equally smitten with, but alas no or none she had heard about.

A girl could always hope though, she sighed almost there, another ten fifteen at the most making me a bit early. Approaching the Wild Horse sign she made the right turn off the blacktop flawlessly, heading up the very long driveway. Hell who was she kidding it is a private road leading to the main ranch house. Ten miles later she pulled up in front of the porch, parked, making her way to the front door it opened, the most striking man she had ever seen stood there waiting for her.

"Hello, you must be Amiela, I'm Logan, Dillon's older brother." He said extending his hand for her to shake.

"Nice to meet you." She mumbled floored by this gorgeous man holding her hand sending thrills zinging through her entire body.

"Come in, welcome." He said ushering her through the massive living room to the kitchen where Dillon was putting the finishing touches on dinner.

"Hi Amiela we're happy you could come." He beamed giving her a quick hug. A first for him to do that but it felt great all the same.

"Wine or?"

"White if you have it, thanks."

She felt stronger now after meeting Logan, Dillon was some what familiar but Logan had sent her for a pussy weeping loop.

Taking the glass Dillon offered she sat at the table beside Logan waiting for Dillon to join her.

The smell of his earthy cologne was making her light headed not to mention she could feel her panties getting wet.

'God how am I going to make it through dinner without soaking my capris.' Red wasn't exactly a colour that hid anything.

Logan took Dillon's cue to throw the steaks on the barbecue, the potatoes and vegetable mix were done, green salad finished waiting in the fridge. And delectable Amiela for dessert spread across the table naked. Dillon came back to the present as she cleared her throat.

"Everything is almost ready, I hope you're hungry?"

"Always, tonight more than most."

Dillon raised his eyebrows at her, he sure wanted her hungry for him!

She realized too late her comment had a double meaning making her blush a pretty pink.

"So how is your project going!"Dillon asked glad he was behind the island, he almost groaned when she licked her lips.

"Great I found evidence today that the pack has maybe fifty members all total. Lots of healthy females to breed and have pups. Plenty of young ones so far this year."

Dillon listened picturing fucking her on all fours, wow do I have it bad or what.I gotta get laid.

"Thats good. So how long do you figure you'll be here?"

"It'll take the rest of this season till the snow flies at least maybe longer."

Logan came back with the steaks overhearing Amiela's last comment.

"So you plan to be around awhile then. I like that alot give us all time to get to know each other."

"I'd like that very much Logan. Dillon you never mentioned you had a brother?"

"Guess I thought I did, but then again everyone around here knows so I don't think of it over much. It just is. Would it have made a difference if I had?"

"Yes it would have, now that I know it certainly changes things for me at least." She hoped he caught on to what she was implying.

"So you would have taken my advances seriously if you had known I had a brother, right?"

"Yes because I want a three way relationship.
 There I said it, I was raised with two fathers as in my mother is married to two men."

"Really, so you are attracted to me then?"

"Yes very much so, and to you as well Logan."

The statement hung there for a moment before Logan responded.

"Well that makes it unanimous then. I've been hard since hello. Dillon and I share our women more than not. We go solo too but we both want one woman to make a commitment to."

"Ok good, where do we go from here?"

"Dinner first, you're going to need all your strength tonight sweaty."Logan replied touching her nose with his finger.

Dillon poured Amiela more wine red this time to go with the steak. Logan filled plates, Dillon set out the salad and condiments on the island asking Amiela how she liked her plate fixed.

Sitting together at the large round table between the brothers gave Amiela delicious wet panties.Her pussy clenched constantly anticipating the evening ahead.

"You mentioned when we first met that you're from Montana which part?"Dillon asked between bites.

"The Front they call it about thirty miles from Butte. Do you know it?"

"Our dad lives in that general area only about fifty miles from Butte, Stanton is only fifteen or so."

"Is he american then?"

"Nope my stepmother is from Stanton originally."

"So why is he down there?"

"My mom died four years ago and he decided to move there, so he bought a ranch, too many memories here, it just kept him sad and grieving."

"Oh, I'm sorry I didn't mean to pry."

"He's doing fine now,Jesse his wife has helped him alot thank god for that woman."Dillon said leaving no doubt he meant it.

"So what brought you to Canada Amiela?"Logan asked changing the subject.

"A grant to do a wolf study in the hopes of transplanting some back to Montana. First though we need to know if they will thrive down there."

"And what have you discovered?"

"They should do well, Montana had a thriving population a hundred years ago then they were exterminated. Food sources exist even now, landscape hasn't changed much, so its a matter of relocation."

"Would you be using ours for transplant?"

"With your permission we could otherwise we have to harvest them off crown land. I have provincial and federal approval if I can prove they will do as well there as they do here.

So it will be a year maybe two before I have all I need to do it."

"We have time with you being close to create something, right Dillon?"

"We all agree to pursue the possibilities of a three way relationship then."

  After the meal was over Logan insisted on taking their wine out to the front veranda to enjoy the sunset.They seated Amiela between them on a wide bench giving her no more room than necessary.

"Do you have any piercings Amiela?"Logan asked in a conversational tone.

"My ears and my belly button. Do you not like them?"

"I love them, we both do."

Dillon nodded his head in agreement.

"If this relationship goes as I think it will we will want your nipples and clit pierced as well, any objections to that?"

"I have thought of it, so no that would be fine with me."

"We're off to a good start then."Logan put his arm around her thinking of the other things he would have done with or without her permission. Meanwhile Dillon held her hand taking solace from her being with them from now on. As the sun splashed into the earth in a most magnificent display of colours Logan nudged Amiela motioning to go inside.As nice as it was he wanted so much more from her on this night.Leading her across the living room to the wide curved staircase they proceeded upward to the master suite they had completely redone after their dad had moved in anticipation of this very day.

"Here we are Amiela now we will truly see how hot and horny we can make each other."Logan stated looking directly into her blue eyes.He wrapped his arms around

her swallowing her up kissing like a man possessed by passion.

"Let me get you out of these clothes,I want you naked now!"

Amiela obliged helping where she could, when she was down to her bra and thong panties Logan stepped back to drink in her perfection.

"Beautiful.I knew you would be."

"I agree." Dillon said coming through the door with a bottle of red wine and three glasses on a tray.

"I waited for you so we can unveil her together."

"Thanks,but it looks like you did a fine job all by yourself."

"Is your slutty little cunt wet and ready for us?"Logan asked pointedly.

"God yes."She replied breathlessly finding the vulgar words turned her on.

"Perfect, have a glass Amiela in celebration of getting laid."

Amiela took the glass drinking deeply,then sheepishly clinked hers with Logan and Dillon's.

Depositing his glass on the table beside the bed Dillon stepped behind Amiela unclasping her bra, smoothed the straps over her arms and off exposing her pert breasts with the large rose nipples to Logan's view.Looking upon her he imagined her tits two sizes bigger, mmmmm she would look fabulous.The rings are going to be perfect on her.

Removing her thong panties Dillon noticed how wet they were and could not resist holding them to his nose inhaling deeply of her essence. He couldn't wait to taste her fragrant pussy.

Leading her to the bed he instructed her to lay in the centre where she could get her first look of him and Logan naked.

Propping herself up on the large pillows she watched as skin light and dark came into view.Both were six foot three and four with muscular chests with a scattering of chest hair narrowing down to two very large cocks.Amiela judged each to be at least ten inches and as fat as a cola bottle. Hmmm I'm in for a treat.

Being a lover of large dicks Amiela looked her fill enjoying herself immensely.Tight buns and eight packs to boot.  How did I end up with these two men,wow.

Logan and Dillon moved onto the bed one either side of Amiela devouring her with their eyes.

Dillon handed the wine glass back to her"Drink up it will relax you.You will need to be as relaxed as possible if you are going to take both of us hon.Have you had anal sex before?"

"Well no, just in my dreams."

"We will be careful,it will hurt some the first time but we will make it as pleasurable as we can.Then we can prepare you for the next time.We like the idea of taking your ass cherry first without any prep.You will come to love it, just as Logan and I do."

Amiela finished her wine handing the glass to Logan who placed it on the bed side table.

Dillon opened the drawer in the night table closest to him and took out two condoms and a tube of lube.

"Now to get that pretty cunt of yours all revved up." Logan said smiling taking a small jar out of the drawer on his side of the bed.Opening it he took a small amount of the white cream on his fore finger and slide it inside her cunt working his finger around a little he removed it. He took another small amount from the jar on his baby finger and massaged it into her clit.

Meanwhile Dillon reached across taking a small amount on his finger wiping it onto the nozzle of the tube of lubricant.

"Ok on your hands and knees with your lovely ass in the air sweetie."

When she was set in her position he wiped her rosette with the remains of the cream on his finger then gently inserted the nozzle in her ass squirting some lube inside.

Satisfied that she was semi relaxed he moved the tube clockwise dispensing the cream evenly.

Logan had been touching her breasts and fondling her clit distracting her by getting her hot for cock.

"How are you feeling?"Logan asked to see the effect of the cream on her,  it would probably take twenty minutes or so to really take a hold.

"It is tingly but nice."

Exactly what he expected to hear.

"Have this Amiela it will help keep you hydrated."Dillon said handing her a glass of mango juice.

After a few minutes she finished the juice handing the glass back to Dillon,she lay back on the pillows. Logan began sucking her nipple while he fingered her pussy hmmm getting nice and hot. Dillon kissed her dueling his tongue with hers while he stroked her rosette dipping his long middle in and out in a mild pumping motion.

Logan moved up to her clit taking her juices with him to ease the way,making small circular motions on the swelling bud.

Dillon left her mouth in favor of her nipple which made her moan and writhe,the cream was a hold of her now making her slutty hot. Amiela felt horny and hot and oh so deliciously wet.Her first orgasm hit her hard leaving her panting.Oh god mmmmmmm ohhhhhhhhh mnhnmmm ahhhhhhhh.

They took their cue,Logan stretched out and positioned Amiela on top nudging her hot slit with the large head of his cock working it and her till he hit home, bottoming out at the mouth of her cervix. Taking her face in his hands he kissed her giving Dillon the access he needed opening her rose.He pushed his long finger into her, hearing her moan.Pulling out he put the head of his cock in place moving forward till the large head disappeared inside her ass.

Logan asked if she was ok and she nodded,Dillon took that as a thumbs up to continue.

Pushing into her virgin ass was hard because she was so tight. Pumping in and out her ring stretched enough making it easier to pump her full of rock hard dick.

Fully seated inside her they gave her a few minutes to get accustomed to the fullness.

"There you are baby,stuffed full of Mclean cock."Dillon gloated smiling.How many times he had envisioned having her ass tight around his dick.

Dillon and Logan set the pace alternating stuffing her.

Amiela screamed after a few thrusts and came working their cocks over with her pussy and ass clenching with abandon. The thrusting increased in tempo as they neared completion,Amiela made sexy noises and screams as she came over and over.  As

Dillon pulled out Logan was still anchored deep inside Amiela riding their orgasmic bliss.

## ~~ Coming Forward~~

All three awoke just as the sun started to shine through the east windows.
"Good morning beautiful, how did you sleep."Dillon asked concern creasing his brow.
"Great,I was exhausted and having you both here made me feel very cozy."
"Are you sore or stiff at all?"
Amiela flexed arms and legs wiggled her fingers.
"No I feel fine."
"Ok then lets go have a shower and then we'll get some breakfast."
Logan followed them into the bathroom arriving as Amiela gave a gasp of delight.Her eyes were glued to the whirlpool tub that held four grown men comfortably.
"I have got to try that out."She laughed as the men gave her an indulgent smile.
"How about later, I'm starved!"Logan offered.
"Ok if I must be quick this morning so you don't faint dead away from hunger, I will."
"Awesome because I want to do wicked things to you."
"Mmmm promise stud?"
Logan just smiled as he stepped into the shower turning on the jets.Oh boy she had no idea how wicked he could be.Amiela followed him into the large luxurious shower and was immediately pinned to the wall,Logan's erection pressed into her tummy, his mouth devouring her.
'He is hungry.'
Tilting her hips toward his erection he plunged into her hot wet sheath taking her breath away with one long stroke.His cock slammed into her cervix and it gave a little.Withdrawing slowly he repeated the stroke feeling her flower open.
'Ahh yes two hot holes.'

Picking up the pace he pounded her into the wall, all Amiela could do was feel it.Wrapping her legs around his waist she went along for the furious ride screaming out her passion to the water cascading over their heads.

Dillon watched his brother fucking Amiela senseless while he shaved thinking how sexy their new lover was and how alluring she would be with a bare pussy devoid of hair and nipple and clit rings.God she would be horny all the time. Going from very little action to a full diet wow a very good change he thought smiling to himself listening to Amiela's moans and shrieks.

Sharing women with Logan had been a very big high for him and now they had one full time,good thing there were two of them to fuck and possess her.

Miss Amiela was in for some surprises with them and she had no idea of what just yet, in time they would apprise her of the details.For now he had some piercings to do today on her lovely tits and clit.

Breakfast was hilarious with Logan and Dillon telling her all about their childhood running wild

around the ranch driving everyone insane especially their mother. She discovered that all the ranch hands but two had been working for the Mclean family their whole careers,two Slim and Ross were second generation ranchers having been raised with Logan and Dillon.In all the ways that counted they were family.

Amiela told them she had two married brothers in a three way relationship and the family highly approved of their choice of a mate.They had three girls and a boy now the little guy Noah being born a couple of months ago.

"Does your sister in law breast feed."Logan wanted to know with a gleam in his eye.

"Yes she does, has with all of them."Amiela answered smiling secretively.

"What's that smile about?"

"Well she says my brothers go crazy for her enlarged milk producing breasts,they can't get enough."She answered blushing.

"Hmm I think we're going to like your brothers.Now its time for your piercings."

Dillon lead the way into the ER as he called it. It was a large medical room in the back of the sprawling ranch house where he mended the many small and sometimes more serious injuries the ranch hands managed to get.

Amiela looked around at the cabinets the gurney with bright lights overhead, a chair that looked like it belonged in a dentist's office. Just your average medical room minus the high tech stuff. Her parents ranch in Montana had a room much the same.

"Ok before we start Amiela I am qualified to do this. My certificate is over there on the wall with all the others. I did this during college to make ends meet. My dads a big believer in contributing to your own life, so no full ticket ride for either of us when we went to school."

"Mine are like that too, worked my tail off in university to get my degree."

"Just take off your clothes and sit down in the chair."

She did as instructed watching Dillon collect the items he needed. Everything was in sterile packages, so disposable she assumed.

Dillon came over adjusting the chair so her legs were raised and open. It kind of reminded her of going to her gynecologist. Touching a peddle he adjusted the lumbar support to thrust her hips out. He did something similar with her shoulders thrusting her tits out at attention.

"Are you comfortable?"

"Yes, I'm fine."

Nodding he opened a vial squeezing a white gel onto first her left nipple then the right. He repeated the procedure on her clit.

Opening a packet he withdrew a hollow tube with a plunger on the end.

Amiela felt her nipples tingle and her clit was too.

"Logan can you get me the rings out of the cabinet above your head?"

"Sure, here they are." Handing them to Dillon he said "All set let's get it done."

Dillon rolled my nipple between his fingers then pulling it slightly he placed the tube to the side and pushed the plunger. I felt a pinch and a heavy gauge needle was through my nipple.Leaving it he did the same with my other one.

Taking a large gold ring he put some cream on the sharp point and eased it through the first nipple he pierced as he backed the needle out.With a click the ring was closed. He did the same with my other nipple,now I was wearing two three inch rings,they were shiny gold with intricate flowers and vines carved into them.

"Amiela how do they feel?"

"Fine, they are lovely.Thank you."

"Ok now for your sweet clit.I can do a horizontal piercing, you are made for it.Would that be ok with you?"

"Yes, ok."

He strapped my thighs to the chair then pierced my clit by plunging the needle so it went under it, then attached a matching ring only slightly smaller.

He touched my clit with a gentle pressure sending my pussy into an immediate orgasm.

"You are extremely sensitive but you will get used to it.

Now I'm going to give you a shot to ward off any infection and put some antibiotic cream onto your piercings.You should be healed in a few days so until then no oral sex."

"Ok."I laughed at his demeanor, and besides he and Logan were the only two I would be having sex with.

When he was finished he unstrapped me and helped me from the chair.

"Get dressed just forget about the bra for the next few days.It will irritate the piercings."

"I was ok with being au naturel,truth be told I did that most of the time anyway."

"I should go back to the trailer,if you tell me what to do with my piercings?"

He came and stood in front of me looking very serious.

"Its best for you to stay here and have me look after them, besides we have just gotten together.I want you to stay with us at least until you're healed.

"Ok,but I will need some clothes and personal items."

"We'll go over so you can get your things."Dillon replied softly stroking my face.

On the way over to my trailer I was sandwiched between Logan and Dillon in Logan's truck.

I was very aware of my new rings every time I moved.

A couple of times I caught looks passing between them that I couldn't decifer.My own brothers did much the same thing so it didn't bother me over much.

It took no time at all to gather what I needed and pack. They looked around outside while they waited for me.

## ~~ **Coming Surprise** ~~

Everyday after my piercings I went to the ER where Dillon attended to them.After a week I was healed or so it seemed to me.
"Ok Amiela just your shot left and we're done."
"I don't think that's necessary its been over a week my piercings feel just fine."
"Infection could still happen,do you want to deal with that?"
"Well no, but couldn't I just take extra care some other way.I really hate shots."
"Not for this no, now be good while I give it to you.Are there any changes in your breasts?"
"Now that you mention it they are harder, firmer.Why?"
"Sometimes women have changes in their breasts with this."Dillon held up the empty syringe.
"Well I feel sexier so it can't be all bad."
"As long as you are happy,that's all that matters."
"It great to finally have a life besides work.I tend to be a workaholic when nothing demands my attention."
"No worries you will be kept busy by Logan and I.Oh and keep going bra less I'll tell you when you can start wearing them again."
"Ok, I prefer going without anyway."
That pleased Dillon,he needed to tell Logan this latest.
"Sweetie why don't you go have that bath you been wanting so much."
"Oh that sounds heavenly."
Dillon left the ER to find Logan,he found him in the kitchen having a coffee.
"Hey bro have I got some good news!"
"What would that be?"
"Amiela likes to go bra less."Dillon crossed his arms and waited.
"That's good,even better than we hoped.Everything is falling into place just perfect.She probably won't even mind when we tell her.Where is Amiela by the way?"
"Having a bath."
"Ok time to get phase two underway.She can have sex now right?"

"Yes good to go."

Dillon washed up to start dinner while Logan went to get the playroom ready for the nights pleasures.

Amiela came into the kitchen looking very refreshed.

"Hey honey how was your bath?"

"Absolutely wonderful, what smells so good?"

Dillon handed her a glass of white wine and motioned for her to sit.

"Chicken, we're having chicken caesars tonight.

"Mmmmm one of my favorites."

Dillon joined her at the table waiting for Logan chatting about places they had been to and places yet to go.

Amiela was wearing her comfy cotton robe at dinner she felt so good after her bath she just couldn't bring herself to get dressed again.

"I like what you're wearing sweetie."Logan drawled as he entered the kitchen.

"Thanks,I just felt like relaxing."

"No complaints here either babe."

Logan and Dillon gave each other a meaningful look that Amiela looking into her wine glass didn't notice.During the meal they were anticipating the evening ahead.Amiela had been given the week to heal but now they could resume her training.

Logan stood holding his hand out "Come with me sweetie there is something I would like to show you."

Amiela took it as he lead her thru the cavernous living room down the wide hall past the study around a corner to a large wooden door with ornate ironwork on it.

"What is this?"She asked surprise in her voice as she had never seen this before. Usually her explorations ended at the study.

"This is our playroom."Logan announced pride obvious in his tone. The apparatus in the room shocked her like the X.The half barrel on legs she had no clue about what it was used for.The sex swing she recognized and blushed.

A large table with restraints she could guess.The many other frameworks who knew and the chains well she could use her imagination.

The large bed obvious.

"Do you like being restrained?"

"Yes I have tried a few things that I liked.I have used a sex swing,been chained with my arms and legs stretched in an X.And tied to a bed with silk ties."

"Good I'm sure you will like the rest and anything new we can devise.But for tonight its the bed we will use."

Dillon came in undressing as he went.

"So what do you think Amiela?"

"Ummm its cool but some of this stuff is a bit daunting.  You aren't into whips I hope?" Uncertainty showing on her pretty face.

"No just feathers and a few mild floggers,they sting a bit but that only heightens one's sexual response."

"We really get off on restraint."Dillon smiled down at her fully naked making her feel very aroused.

"Let me help you out of this."Dillon took her robe off and laid it aside.

Taking her hand he led her to the bed.

"Just lay on your back in the center."

Amiela crawled to the middle of the bed and lay down.

Dillon took her wrist kissed it then cuffed her while Logan did the same to the opposite ankle.Then proceeded to cuff her wrist while Dillon cuffed her opposite ankle.

Dillon flipped a switch on the wall at the head of the bed making her ankles rise and spreading her legs wide. Now fully bared for their inspection.

Dillon climbed onto the bed going for her pussy dildo in hand,Logan kissed her then lay beside her totally nude, Amiela felt her pussy dampen from the site.

Dillon lowered his mouth to her cunt licking softly making her moan.Flicking his tongue over her ring made it dance,Amiela bucked in her bonds seeking more.

 Logan feasted on her nipples gorging himself on her flesh working her rings to drive her to the brink.As she came hard Dillon drove the dildo into her hot pussy pumping in and out of her till she went limp.

Positioning the head of his cock at her slick hot slit he sunk into her wet depths while Logan sucked her nipples hard until she came, he tasted the first rich creamy burst of milk on his tongue.Finishing milking her breast he and Dillon switched places repeating driving her wild to orgasm yet again until Dillon tasted her sweet nectar draining her breast.

"Mmm that was delicious sweetie,I cannot wait till there's more."Logan proclaimed.

Coming around after her soul shattering orgasms she asked "More what?"

"Milk babe, you're lactating."

"What, how on earth can I be doing that!"

"I don't know sweetie,but you are and I loved sucking you dry."He knew, but they wanted her to love it before they disclosed everything.For now they would give her the chance,and keep training her to give milk when she orgasmed.Nothing like being buried in pussy and tasting milk.

Dillon un-shackled her,then they all got in the huge playroom tub each taking turns washing and fondling their new mare.

## ~~Coming Together~~

Amiela was sleeping soundly when Dillon and Logan left their bed as the morning lightened only slightly.
They went to their individual rooms showered dressed and met back in the kitchen.
"So, that went ok last night.No freaking out or anything. How much should we tell her?"Dillon asked looking concerned.
"We should give here a chance to like being our sexy slutty little brood mare before we disclose anything.In the mean time you should give her the hormones in her juice or something just so she doesn't get suspicious."
"Can do.Maybe I'll give her breakfast in bed this morning."Dillon said rubbing his hands together.
"How soon should we milk her again?"
"Not until tonight at least.She'll produce more as time goes on but for now we'll only get slightly more than last night."
"How long till full production do you think?"
"A week at least."
"So say in two three weeks she will be producing the maximum amount she is equipped for."
"Yep, so we can decide who gets it when we know the amount.Nothing wrong with giving away a taste though.
"I think we need to train her a little more first, after all we want her to have the best possible experience.There are a few misconceptions there yet,she needs to feel totally free before we share anything."
"Keeping her to ourselves is fine by me."
"Ok I will see you at breakfast."Logan left with a smile on his face and a spring in his step.
Dillon made coffee had a couple of cups and made breakfast.Loading a tray for Amiela he turned to find her standing in the kitchen door smiling to herself.

"Well good morning, how do you feel?"

"Pretty good, no more milk and my breasts feel fine."

Dillon could tell by looking at her breasts that they had increased over the past week by one full cup size however he kept this info to himself.

"I was going to bring you breakfast in bed but you can eat it here." Amiela crossed the kitchen sitting down at the table preparing to eat.She was starving this morning.

Leaning over she gave Dillon a searing kiss.

"You know I wouldn't mind if we went back to bed."
Amiela flirted shamelessly.

Dillon smiled at her wrapping his arms around her sexy body."You know there are other places we can fuck,like right here on this table. Its the perfect height for me to plow that sweet pussy of yours."

Drawing back he saw lust in her eyes.

"I can go for that."

"That lovely cunt a little hungry?"He asked teasing her.

"Ravenous is more like it."

Dillon knew one of the lovely side benefits of the hormones he had been giving her was an ever increasing sex drive,add to that the rings and presto one horny, slutty little mare for the taking anytime.

Picking her off the chair he set her on the edge of the table dropping her robe, baring her.

"You are beautiful baby,I could watch you walk around naked all day."

"Fuck me please."

Dropping his pants he thrust into her bottoming out at her cervix.She wrapped her legs around him leaning back slightly to give him deeper penetration.

"That's it honey, yes, yes, yes mmmmmmm."She panted.

Dillon thrust harder, faster plunging deep into her womb over and over. He felt her orgasm begin which triggered his own filling her to overflowing with his hot creamy cum.

Holding her while she flew apart in his arms. Shuddering through the last ripples of her orgasm.Amiela snuggled into him so perfectly he reluctantly let her go when his cock softened out of her tight pussy.

"I will never look at this table the same way again."He chuckled.

"I'm much better now,thank you Dillon that was Amazing!"

"My absolute pleasure."

Kissing her softly he helped Amiela off the table and into her robe. Amiela left Dillon in the kitchen cleaning up while she went to have a shower and get dressed.

Leaving the bedroom in a white tank top and short shorts she made her way down the grand curving staircase to the study where she had work waiting.She had received the results of the samples she had collected now they needed to be studied and logical conclusions drawn.  Immersed in her work she had no idea of the time until Logan popped his head in the door.

"Care for some lunch?"

"That time already, ok this will keep till later."

They found Dillon grilling burgers with all the fresh toppings prepared sitting on the table.

Remembering what she and Dillon had done on said table made her blush scarlet.Logan either didn't notice or chose to say nothing which she was grateful for.

Dillon came through the back door with a plate of burgers and buns all ready.

Logan took plates out of the cupboard setting them on the table.

"Did you get any work done Amiela?"

"Yes quite a lot.I'm surprised how quickly time flew by but it is what usually happens when I start analyzing test results."

"Tonight we'll take your mind off all of that with a cozy night in."

"What are you up to Dillon?"

"Its a surprise,so you just have to wait."

"Oh really, maybe I'll just work then."

"Nope we'll just come get you and carry you kicking and screaming if necessary!"

She begged off dinner professing she wanted to finish up,by nine o'clock she had two large men carrying her up the stairs not willing to wait any longer.

They set her feet on the floor in the middle of the bedroom.
"Now Amiela we have given you lots of time to work now you are all ours."Logan stated in a firm tone telling her she would do as they said.Dillon opened the huge walk in closet went inside and came out with a sheer red gossamer robe.
"Put this on please."He asked softly.
Undressing under their lustful gaze excited her, she felt her pussy slick in as she removed her underwear.Taking the confection from his outstretched fingers she slipped it on.It was silk so smooth it whispered against her skin making her nipples poke out against the fabric as she slide the two buttons through their holes between her breasts.Logan turned her around by the shoulders so she could look at the image she made in the mirror.She saw her body through the robe accentuated by light and shadow.
"You look lovely and oh so fuckable."Dillon said approvingly,getting his brother's agreement by a nod of his head.
Amiela felt very sexy and alluring she wondered what they had in mind now?
Each taking a hand they led her from the room to the living room where candles were lit casting the room in a sensual glow,leading to the sofa where they indicated she sit.On the coffee table sat a tray with a bottle of excellent wine and three glasses.
"Now that we have your attention and you definitely have ours, we would like to propose a toast to the most beautiful woman to grace our home and our lives.Thank you Amiela for deciding to become our love."Logan said and Dillon agreed.
"I second that.Thank you."
 Over the wine they discussed the present and the future.
Amiela said she wanted to take a trip to Australia and New Zealand when her wolf study was complete.Logan and Dillon thought that would be a marvelous vacation and planned to go with her when the time came.
"We want you in the playroom now."Logan said leaving no doubt in her mind it was an order.She was finding Logan was very commanding on occasion, when he ordered her she found it exciting not to mention stimulating.

"Ok, whatever the two of you have in mind I hope you know I need to cum."

That was music to their ears because she would cum a lot before this night was over.

"Come along sweetie,we will take care of you."Dillon replied in his soft sexy voice she never seemed to be able to resist.

Stepping into the playroom they each took a wrist walked her to the X frame cuffing her to it. Logan spread her left leg out and cuffed her ankle while Dillon did her right.The robe she wore opened from below her breasts to the floor exposing her front to their view.

Dillon unbuttoned the flimsy fabric parting it to the sides of her breasts which had grown noticeably since that morning he noted.Perhaps she would be in full production by the end of the week.Logan had noticed she was much bigger licking his lips in anticipation of the warm creamy milk to come.

While Dillon retrieved the dildos they planned to use Logan stroked her perfect tits, running his hand across her nipples they hardened.Amiela moaned at the  contact telling him she was very sensitive.Snaking his hand down her abdomen to her pussy she shivered delighting him. Dipping his two fingers just inside her slit he found her lubricated, taking his wet fingers he circled her clit gently flicking her ring experimentally to gauge her reaction Amiela screamed in pleasure writhing in her bonds as the orgasm took hold.

Dillon handed the twelve inch dildo to Logan so he could thrust it inside her cunt keeping the lubed dildo to ease into her pretty ass.Amiela felt the dildos thrust up inside her body but didn't care.Dillon affixed the small thong like harness onto her to keep the dildos in place, taking the remotes in hand he turned both on watching her spiral into another orgasm.

"Rim her nipples with your tongue Logan,that should stimulate the flow then on her next cum we can milk her."

Logan always relished training a filly to milk and Amiela was one prize he intended to enjoy.He tasted the first drop leaving her till she came.

They watched as she came down off her orgasm slumping in her cuffs.The dildos vibrated away inside her feeling delicious making her build to the next one.

Dillon lifted her head kissing her lips while Logan touched her clit through the thin harness that covered it making her squirm.As soon as her orgasm began they each latched onto a nipple suckling till her milk

came in flowing into their mouths in warm streams.She shook in her cuffs for long minutes before it waned off.

They had drained each breast in the process very satisfied with the quantity and the quality was

ambrosia the most perfect they had ever tasted, their milk loving friends would be over the moon about their sweet Amiela.

Dillon took the harness and dildos away cleaning everything then stored them back in their slots in the cabinet.

Taking her off the X frame Logan carried her upstairs to their bed where he bathed her with a wash cloth,patting her dry with a soft towel then covered her with the quilt just as Dillon came in.

"How is she?"

"Out of it, she was asleep when I carried her up here."

"Not much wonder after three powerful orgasms and giving two quarts of milk."Dillon remarked.

"Is she in full production then?"

"Not yet,I expect she'll produce close to a gallon a day."

"We'll have to use the machine for that.Maybe we should try her on that next?"

"At the next milking.Lets see if she fills out again as she did today then we can otherwise it will be a few days yet."

"Hopefully she responds positively to milking."Logan remarked wanting her to love producing a most precious elixir for them.

Amiela awoke in the middle if the night to find her men snuggled up to her.It was too dark to see them but feeling was good enough.A memory flashed of them suckling her breasts giving her the most fantastic prolonged orgasm of her life.She felt her breasts through the silk finding them sensitive to her touch and very firm.

Drifting off to sleep she vaguely remembered Dillon saying something about milking.

## ~~Coming In~~

The men climbed out of bed at first light to get their various jobs done so they could spend the day with Amiela.Given it was sunday made chores light as most of the horses were out to pasture.
The stallions needed to be cared for and two mares with foals.
 Finishing up they headed back to the house just as the sun made its appearance.
Grabbing a coffee from the pot they sat down at the table waiting for Amiela to come down.
"Do you think she realized we milked her last night?" Logan asked with raised eyebrows.
"I don't know she was a little delirious during her third orgasm and each one was more powerful than the previous one."
"Suppose we will find out when she gets up."Logan sighed anticipation making him impatient for results.
"I'll get breakfast ready,hopefully she'll be up by the time its done."
"Better yet I will go and see if she's up and if not perhaps a little morning fuck is in order to bring her around." Logan said smiling giving his impatience an outlet.
Dillon laughed at his back on his way out the door.
Logan listened intently for any sound from Amiela on his way up the stairs and down the hall to the master suite.
Pausing at the door he admired her lying on her back her breasts sitting on her chest much bigger than the night before. A large D cup for sure and by the looks of them they needed to be milked again.She was responding to the treatment much better than they had originally thought she might.
Stripping he climbed in bed caressing her tits admiring the size and hardness.Parting her legs he slipped a finger inside her pussy hmmm wet and ready.

Guiding his huge rod he gently pushed the head inside making her moan.Encouraged he thrust harder stretching her tight channel forcing her to accept him all the way into her luscious body.Fully seated he rocked back and forth teasing her cervix to open letting his huge cock own her womb.It flowered slightly allowing the bulbous head to lodge itself, forcing her to open fully.One more thrust brought him to the sweet spot he craved like nothing else. Amiela opened her eyes to find Logan smiling down upon her with his dick buried to the hilt.

"Good morning baby."He said kissing her ravenously, she responded in kind spreading her legs out and back to give him space to fuck her hard.

'Hmmmmmm this is the way to wake up.Fuck me Logan hard please."

"My pleasure sweetie."He replied moving upon her thrusting into her pussy bottoming out pounding her

into the mattress over and over until she came screaming her release in his ear.

In the aftermath of their shared bliss Logan noticed his cheek was wet where it lay against Amiela's breast. Raising his head quickly looking down it was leaking milk.Getting off the bed he went to the bathroom for a cloth to tidy her up and himself.Coming back he noticed she looked a bit shocked.

"What's the matter?"He asked softly concerned by the look on her pretty face.

"I'm leaking milk,I thought this was a one time thing like my hormones got a little out of whack and would correct themselves.But Nooo I'm fully lactating now!"

"Don't worry Dillon and I will fix it for you."Logan soothed her, wiping her breasts and between her legs gently.

Retrieving a fresh thigh length wrap from the closet he held it up coaxing her to come and put it on.

She crawled across the huge ocean of a bed sliding onto the floor.Turning her back to Logan she put her arms through the short cap sleeves of the wrap wincing slightly as it brushed her sensitive nipples. Closing the front snap between her breasts she was ready to see Dillon and find out this solution they had in mind.

Coming September 2013

Coming Home Dillon's Destiny

The second book in the Coming Home Series

~ ~ ~ ~

Coming January 2014

Coming Home Amiela's submission

The third book in the Coming Home Series

**Coming Home Dillon's Destiny Book Two**
Copyright 2013 Adeline Moore
Author: Adeline Moore

Paperback book published in Canada.
ISBN:9780991959358
Cover art by: A.R.M.

Dedication
Believe in your dreams because they do come true

# Contents

## Chapter One Coming On

Amiela entered the kitchen ahead of Logan looking none too pleased with the new turn of events.  She was lactating heavily if her estimation was correct.

"What's wrong?" Dillon asked anxiously hoping she would stay calm.

Ripping open her wrap she replied between clenched teeth "This is wrong!"

Ok so much for loving it Logan grimaced at the force of her anger toward them.

"We can fix it, I promise you will feel much better afterward. Come with me!" Dillon commanded having none of her outburst this morning.  She had been producing for a few days now, its not like this was the first time.Leading her down a short hall off the kitchen they entered a bright airy room with windows that looked toward the mountains in the distance.  It was a beautiful sight which calmed Amiela immediately.

"Better now? " Dillon asked in a calm voice he used to settle skittish horses.

"Yes, how can you fix this?". She gestured helplessly toward her large inflated breasts.

"We have to milk you." Letting that sink in he moved over to a cabinet that ran from the floor to the ceiling, opening the door Amiela saw it was a large closet.

Dillon stepped inside pushing something out on wheels covered by a white cloth.

"Ok Logan and I have milked you several times now, but given the amount you have we will have to use a machine to express all of it." Saying that he lifted the covering off to Amiela's gasp of dismay.

"What is that?"

"Its a milking machine, this one is only for women. See here the cups are properly sized for your nipples. I attach these onto your breasts, the plastic tubes run down to this bottle. You sit here he motioned to a seat, your legs go in the grooves here, he pointed to shallow indentations in the legs of the chair, your hands go here flat on the arms. Dillon sat demonstrating how she would position herself.

"Come here and we will make you feel better." Dillon commanded softly, leaving no doubt in Amiela's mind he meant it.

Walking over to him she noticed underneath the seat was closed, like a box had been built under it.

"What's under the seat in that?" Pointing to the box.

"The workings for the machine, nothing to concern yourself with. All you need to do is sit and enjoy the feelings when your milk is expressed. It will be wonderful, you'll see."

He was so happy and confident Amiela couldn't help feeling ok about all this. Logan was standing by the door smiling waiting for her to do as instructed. Sitting down Dillon took her robe off then strapped her left wrist to the chair arm then her right.

Logan was kneeling putting cuffs around her ankles, that done he put the cups on her nipples while Dillon fastened the straps behind her back to hold them in place. Looking down she noticed a thin strap ran between the cups in front between her breasts as well.

"Ok now I'm going to turn the machine on." Dillon held a small remote in his hand, pushing a button the milking machine started to hum, there was a squeezing sensation and a suction she could feel on her nipples. Looking down she could see her nipples were sucked into long round tubes attached to the cups on her breasts. The machine was stretching her nipples out away from her rings. Having her breasts sucked triggered her pussy to get very wet. 'Oh god I can't cum like this.'

"I think you're ready for a nice hot cock up your pussy so your milk lets down. You always produce more when you're being fucked and sucked sweetie." Logan declared smugly.

A door in the seat slide away then a giant dildo touched her pussy lips, Logan reached down spreading her lips so the cock could enter her. Gasping at the sensation of a warm cock about to fuck her Amiela turned wild eyes on the brothers.

"You will love this just go with it." Dillon soothed stroking her head of shiny soft hair.

The cock moved up inside expanding her pussy walls as it inched in, fully seated it began plunging in and out in firm even strokes. Mmmmmmmhnnnmm oooooh ohhh she moaned feeling milk being expelled from her breasts.

"There now thats better good steady flow, I bet our little mare feels really good getting fucked and sucked. Look how wet her hot slutty cunt is, its dripping Dillon, have you ever seen anything sexier than this?"

"Nope our Amiela is everything we could wish for and more. We may have to milk her twice a day from now on. I hope you're gonna be ok with that? Lactating tends to make mares very slutty, they need to be fucked all the time."

"Nnnnnmmmmmmmmmmm ohhhhhh oh oh ohhhhhhhhhh mmmmmmmmmmmm."

"Seems like she loves her new fuck buddy maybe try the bigger one next that jets semen Dillon."

"Thats the next step anyway, then we will make introductions."

"This should break down those silly hang ups she has."

Dillon turned the dildo speed up so it pounded into her pussy sending her over the edge into a massive orgasm sending milk gushing down the tubes to capacity. He maintained the speed to send her spiraling toward another one.

"Logan can you call and tell Slim to come and make breakfast, I will finish up here then we will join you."

"Ok will do." Logan left walking into the kitchen to find Slim already fixing a nice big breakfast.

"Don't forget Amiela's juice and add the hormones."

Slim's eyes lit up "so you're lactating her then, Ross and I wondered if you would."

"Yep we are, she makes a grade A milk. We'll have them knocking down the door for it once they get a sample. You going to be around this weekend we're planning a little party for Amiela."

"I won't miss that little filly giving us a taste."

"Good they should be along directly, Dillon was just finishing up her first machine milking."

"How did she take that?"

"Fine she seems to like the cock, makes her produce more."

"Nothing like watching a woman being rammed full of cock and being milked.Its been a long time since we had fresh breast milk."

Amiela and Dillon walked into the kitchen, he seated her at the table handing her the orange juice. She drank gratefully.

"How did you like your milking?" Logan asked expectantly.

"It was good, makes me soo horny and thirsty."

"Any problem with continuing?"

"No I'm fine with it, I've never had so many hard monster orgasms before."

"Great I knew you would love it."

"You are our sexy little mare now, you will beg to get fucked. Lactating does that, makes you slutty hot."

"How long will I lactate for?"

"For as long as we want you to."

"What are you talking about!" She raised her voice to a screech.

"Dillon and I want you lactating providing milk for us and a group of friends who have a breast milk fetish. You produce the finest milk we have ever tasted. So you will keep all of us supplied, understand?" Logan gave his command and that was that.

"I understand." Amiela replied submissively.

She may not like it now but she would come around to it he knew this instinctively.

"Amiela you will have to be milked tonight, you gave three quarts this time but that will improve as time goes by."

Amiela just sat and listened in her short wrap. Dillon put some eggs, bacon and toast on a plate and set it in front of her.

"You need to eat to keep your strength up. Then perhaps a nice bath and I need to remove your pussy hair so it doesn't irritate you. I have time to do that after breakfast."

Dillon had some cream to use on her tits to keep them firm and elastic. She also needed a full prep of stimulant this kept her lactating efficiently and horny. Both of those facts pleased him.

Amiela was having mixed feelings to lactating, on the one hand she loved the fierce orgasms she had when they milked her either manually or mechanically. Her tits were much fuller now, she doubted any of her bras or tops would fit.  Now Dillon was saying they would get even bigger.

"I'll measure your bust line so I know how big you are.Cup size is a nice D right now that will expand to at least a double maybe triple D as your production goes up."

Gasping Amiela felt as though he were reading her mind.

"None of my tops are going to fit at this rate. I'll have to go shopping."

"No need for that there is a whole wardrobe of clothes for you upstairs in the master suite.  I will show you later."

"Ok, I will take a look." She replied quietly. Grumping to herself they had better be really nice clothes.

"Come along Amiela time to get you prepared.  I want that pussy hair gone, you will feel so much better afterward."

Entering the ER Dillon collected everything he would need to make Amiela's pussy bare and silky.

"Get up on the table and place your legs in the stirrups."

Once she was settled on the padded table he adjusted the stirrups spreading her legs wide then strapping them down. Moving behind her head he took each hand cuffing them to a bar just behind.

"I'm going to explain things to you, the substance I use won't hurt at all, it will tingle and when I'm done the hair on your pussy will be gone, in six months I will repeat the process thereby making it permanent. I'm going the do your legs and underarms as well. Also I will give you a injection to keep you comfortable while you are lactating.  And lastly I will moisturize your entire body after your bath to keep your skin supple.  Oh and I will be putting nipple expanders on you, they will help lengthen your nips and you will wear these until the desired results have been achieved."

"How long do you want my nipples to be?"

"Two inches will do it.  That will be a nice peg to latch onto to milk you and the machine will help keep them nice and long."

"I don't know about all this, I don't think I want my nipples any bigger."

"Trust me when the procedure is complete you will love it. You already love the orgasms you get don't you?"

She didn't answer just nodded her head slightly.

"Ok then you just leave it all in my hands I will make sure you love being a slutty little mare. We want you to be happy and free in your sexual life so just enjoy what's happening."

Dillon knew she would become exactly what they wanted it was her nature to submit to strong men, hell she had been born for it. The more she experienced with their guidance the more she would crave it.

Applying the oily cream to her pussy he did the same with her legs and underarms, taking a disposable cloth he wiped the cream and hair away, feeling her mound it was as smooth as a newborn. Running the cloth down each side of her slit made her moan and writhe. Her pussy was sopping wet, fingering her cunt she came screaming in ecstasy . He finished her legs and underarms then un-strapped and inspected the backs of her legs for any hair. Satisfied he un-cuffed her hands helping her from the table.

"Lets go get you in the bath then I will moisturize you."

"That sounds really... Good to me. Will you join me?"

"Best offer I've had today sweetie. Watching you on the milking machine got me going, would you be ok with getting fucked again?"

"Oh god yes, let's go. Amiela tugged his hand then took off running her big tits bouncing wildly for the bathroom in the master suite. Dillon followed his long strides catching up with her at the bedroom door catching her around the waist swinging her up into his arms carrying her into the bathroom where he set her down on her feet.

Turning the taps on the tub he let the water run while he found the bubble bath he wanted, pouring some in the tub the bubbles started to rise with the water.

Stripping his clothes off he took Amiela's wrap admiring her big globes touching them gently he bent down to latch onto her nipple. Two strong pulls on her teat and her creamy milk flooded his mouth, he suckled strongly for several minutes then left her to step into the massive tub built for four grown men.

"Come I'll suck your other titty once you're in here."
She climbed in settling back on the padded side, Dillon massaged her breasts until she was moaning, sliding his fingers into her pussy slit he found her ready to go. Placing his cock at her entrance he plowed ahead bottoming out at her cervix. Latched onto her nipple he sucked hard getting her tit to squirt into his mouth. Amiela brought her knees up to either side of her tits wanting Dillon to pound her cunt deeper, he thrust forward a few more inches hitting the small opening in her cervix driving his huge cock head into her womb. She was delirious with orgasmic fever wanting more, Dillon kept sucking and thrusting to her cries until he pumped his seed into her. When she quieted he withdrew moving her in between his legs stroking her body relaxing into the quiet serenity only a thorough fucking can give.

 Exiting the tub Dillon dried every inch of her with care, he then applied his special moisturizer with the sexual stimulant in it that would keep Amiela sexually ravenous for the weekend. It always took a few days to reach its full effect if applied daily for three days. It had done wonders making her tits firm.
Throwing a robe on Dillon took Amiela's hand leading her into the bedroom, opening the dressing room he showed her all the clothes she had to wear.
"Where did all these come from and when?".
She was completely mesmerized by all the colours and styles that she could see on the front racks. Everything totally suited her to a tee.
"Personal shopper, yours by the way. I will give you all his info later. Greg is at your disposal whenever you require his assistance."
"Ok I can get used to this!" She nodded her head in the affirmative.
"Great, I'm glad you like what you've seen so far everything can be returned if you don't like something. Now how about this top?"
Dillon had picked a royal blue silk tank top with a plunging cleavage showing neckline. He paired that with white shorts and royal blue beaded sandals.

"Undies are in the drawers over there. This has a built in bra so you won't need one."

"Ok, I like the outfit. Thank you."

"Get acquainted with your new wardrobe I have to run, I have an appointment arriving soon." He gave her a mind numbing kiss, dressed and left.

~~~~

# Coming Home Coming Introduction

 Amiela spent the morning perusing her wardrobe she found everything from casual to formal evening wear all to accommodate her larger bust line.  She thought about changing her shorts as they were a bit short now that she had been bending and stretching in them,  looking in the mirror standing straight she could almost see the crease where her leg met her buttocks. The top was nice even though it showed a lot of cleavage and the swell of her breast on either side of the V neckline.  She decided to leave her outfit as is, leaving the bedroom heading to the kitchen in search of lunch.

Entering the kitchen she found Slim busy with a huge lunch, baked ham, scalloped potatoes, green and yellow beans, fresh bread and a fruit cobbler for dessert, all set out waiting for everyone to arrive.

"Everyone should be her in a minute or two have a seat make yourself comfortable." He said handing her a glass of iced tea.

She turned toward the men's voices as four entered the kitchen. Logan and Dillon she knew, who were they?

"Amiela we would like you to meet Cloudwalker and his brother Clouddancer.  Gentlemen this is our girlfriend Amiela."

Extending her hand to the native men she managed shyly."Nice to meet you both."

"And you."The two native men replied in unison.

"Sit gentlemen we will eat and you and Amiela can get to know each other." Logan said in a commanding tone.

"Amiela, Dillon tells me you are a biologist studying the wolf population in the area in hopes of transplanting a few to Montana." Cloudwalker ventured.

"Yes I am, so far its taken five years to gather the data I will need to do it, it will take another two of studying the pack here to make a convincing case so the powers at be will sign final approval for the transplant."

"Large endeavor for one person."

"Well. Yes and no I have a team now they will all be here next year after I do all the ground work. What do you do?"

"I'm a scientist, I study females of two species at the moment."
Turning to Clouddancer she asked the same question.

"I'm a OBGYN. My practice is in town, I imagine we will see each other on a professional basis one day."

He said it so matter of factuality it took Amiela a minute to get what he was saying.

"Possibly doctor but not before the wolf transplant is concluded."
She didn't have control over her breasts lactation but having children she would say when. Looking from Logan to Dillon she pushed the point with a stubborn look that said you got that boys! From the looks she received she knew they were going to have a discussion in the near future.

Cloudwalker looked around him and knew his friends were in deep shit if they pushed her to have a baby now.

Oh well not his problem he only needed a blood test from her to study the effects of lactation on her system.

Clouddancer cleared his throat hoping to ease the tension by saying "Totally understandable given how long you have been working toward this goal. So where are you from?"

"Montana my family have a ranch there."

"Nice country down there."

"Yes and to hear wolves howling there would make it perfect. At least for me."

"Would you mind giving me a blood sample before we leave?"
Cloudwalker asked.

"I suppose I could do that but why me?"

"Your lactating, that's one thing I'm researching."

Amiela looked from Dillon to Logan furious "You told a stranger my very personal affliction! HOW dare you, its nobody's business!"

With that she rose and stomped from the room red faced and humiliated. Grabbing her keys and purse off the hall table she ran to her truck before the tears engulfed her.

Starting it she gunned it down the ranch road that led to the highway. With no place in mind to go to she drove aimlessly finding herself at her fifth wheel trailer. Now what she asked herself. They were damn well going to apologize or she would pull up stakes find another wolf pack and leave those two in her dust.

She realized she was starving as she had left her lunch behind with the two jackasses, looking in the cupboard she found some tomato soup and crackers that would do till she went to town for supplies because she was not going back to the ranch house any time soon, lactation or not she would figure out a way to relieve the pressure.

"We well and truly fucked that up!" Dillon said sarcastically.

"Yep you sure did, she doesn't know about the hormone cocktail does she?" Cloudwalker accused them.

"No we wanted her to love it so much it wouldn't matter but after today I think we better keep it to ourselves if we value her."

"And your balls."

"Them too. Man I still can't believe she exploded like that, she's been so submissive all the way through."

"Dillon, Clouddancer and I are strangers to her, I can see her not wanting outsiders to know about her affliction as she put it. I know it was embarrassing not to mention humiliating for her to have me ask for the sample and then she finds out I know about the lactation. Good luck getting around her on this one. Groveling would be best I think if you expect her to give you another chance."

"When is she due to be milked next?" Clouddancer asked.

"This evening around five."

"I have a breast pump in my medical supplies in the truck, if you have any idea where I can find her I will drop it off on my way home."

"Her trailer's at the green spring that's the only place I know of unless she decided to go home to Montana she could be halfway

to the border by now." Dillon's frustration and anger were understandable but missed placed in Clouddancer's opinion.
"I'll let you know if I find her, but know this if she asks for my help in drying her breasts I will help her."
"Understood." Logan, Dillon and Cloudwalker said in unison. Clouddancer left shortly after, leaving the three to figure out a way to get back in Amiela's good graces.
"Could this day get any more fucked up!" Logan exploded.
"It could if she knew about the cocktail, thank god she doesn't or she would be headed to the border away from us." Dillon replied dismally.
"We have to cancel the weekend festivities, there's no way she'll trust us again for awhile." Logan mused almost to himself.
"Well I should get going too, let me know if I can do anything to help." With that Cloudwalker let himself out the front door and headed for his truck.
A hour later Dillon's cell rang picking it up he said "Hello did you find her?"
"Her truck is at the trailer but no sign of Amiela. She may have not wanted to answer the door but I got the feeling she was out somewhere. I left the breast pump with my card on the step so she'll get it when she returns. I would leave her be for awhile, let her deal with things in her own way.  I should be by here in a day or two so I'll check on her then."
"Ok thanks Clouddancer we appreciate everything you've done."
"Talk to you later."
 For the next two days nothing was heard from Amiela, taking their friends advice Logan and Dillon stayed away from the green spring hoping she would call.
At noon over lunch on the third day they were ready to go storm the trailer and bring her back kicking and screaming if necessary then Dillon's phone rang.
"Hey Clouddancer have you seen her?"
"Yep we're having lunch as we speak.  She wants you two to come by for a chat, her words. Now if you can get away? Ok I will tell her."
"So they agreed to come I assume?"

"Ya they'll be here in half an hour or so."

"Ok good, I hate leaving things dangling."

"Give them hell they both deserve it!"

"Oh, I plan to."

Clouddancer liked the evil look on Amiela's face, served both Dillon and Logan right for divulging private information without asking her first.

"Good, I'm going but if you would rather I stayed I will?"

"Its ok I will call you later."

"Thanks for lunch, it was great.". He said rising from the table in the fifth wheel unfolding his long frame, giving Amiela a hug he left stepping down onto the ground his boots crunching on the grass. She stood at the door waving goodbye as he pulled the truck around heading for the main road.

Logan and Dillon arrived shortly after Clouddancer left pulling to a stop beside the fifth wheel.

Amiela came outside sitting down in one of the lawn chairs."You made it, now have a seat." She motioned to two chairs a distance away from the one she was occupying. She needed distance right now and to hell with them if they didn't like it!

Both sat down obeying her wishes.

"Now firstly you two had no fucking right discussing me with anyone and Not someone I don't even know! How dare you think that would be ok with me you jackasses.

If I ever forgive you, you will be damned lucky and if and when I decide to have a child That will be my dam choice Not yours.  Got that! Now on to this lactation business don't think for one minute I didn't know you two were up to something.  Doing this without my consent is abhorrent. How dare you decide for Me!"

Feeling better by the minute getting this off her chest was pure pleasure.  Logan and Dillon looked rather sick.  Good you deserve it she thought.

"I do know how to reverse this, whether I do or not is up to me!"

Getting an opening to speak Logan asked " So have you reversed it Amiela?"

"No, and I dumped the milk down the drain."

"Ok, do you want to continue with it?"

"I will for one month, renewable if I choose."

"I can live with that, what else should we know?"

"No more potions or anything without my consent, I will walk away from you if I have to."

"Ok deal."

"Are you willing to come back home with us so we can hammer all the details out there?" Dillon asked quietly.

"Yes, I have some things to finish here, I will meet you there in a couple of hours."

With that said they left a bit shell shocked by her forceful attitude they had not seen before, she had always been so agreeable but then again everyone had their limits she has just shown them a few of hers. The hormones she would have to continue along with the other therapy they had introduced her to, whether she liked it or not, she had agreed to another month so perhaps they could delay telling her everything for awhile yet and in the meantime she would grow to love it they hoped.

Logan grabbed a couple of beers out of the refrigerator upon their arrival home handing one to Dillon he
asked "So how much do we tell her?"

"We cop to the hormone therapy but not to the injections or the creams. That way if she refuses it we can always continue the others because she won't lactate if she doesn't have most of them."

"Ok, and the reasoning is because we like the breast milk, not knowing about the buyers right now is a good thing, let her get used to milking before she knows all the facts."

Dillon nodded in agreement hoping this meeting with Amiela went well, he could not see a life without her in it, pulling a long drink out of his beer he relaxed a little letting the alcohol work on his frayed nerves.

As much as the brothers hated waiting they did just that relieved when she came walking into the kitchen exactly on time wearing a pair of tight faded jeans and a tank top sky blue matching her eyes.

Amiela had a stern serious look on her face her eyes boring into the brothers like she wanted to extract every thought from their minds. Sitting down at the table her mind wandered back to the morning she had sex with Dillon a few feet away.  Blushing slightly making eye contact with Logan she said evenly. "Tell me what did you put in my drinks to cause this?" She held her large breasts up. "A hormone cocktail developed by Cloudwalker to induce lactation." Logan held her gaze challenging.

"Ok its what I thought, my second option, at first I thought maybe my hormones were off kilter. I can get Clouddancer to reverse this, he said he would if I wanted him to. I think for now I will try the milking for the month to see if its something I can tolerate. Do I have to keep taking the hormones and how big will my girls get?" Dillon spoke up "Its best if you do and probably a double D, I don't expect any more than that. Cloudwalker still needs that blood sample from you."

Amiela sat a bit stunned they were being so honest with her, it changed her view back to her original thoughts of them.

"He can come by any time and get one for his research. The double D ok not so bad.  Thank you for being straight with me about this. Now do we have any wine?"

She smiled for the first time in three miserable days away. Logan went to the fridge and poured her a large glass of white wine, setting it in front of her.

"Are we forgiven and can we get on with our relationship?" He asked nicely with a hopeful look on his chiseled face.

"Yes your are and yes we can I'm here to stay."

Logan got to her first gathering her in his arms for a starved passionate kiss, Dillon followed suit leaving no doubt in her mind that she was wanted and needed.

Throwing her over his shoulder he walked through the house her breasts bobbing up and down on his back, her clit rubbing on his shoulder sending delicious tremors through her pussy. He dropped her in a heap on the playroom bed, looking like a hungry tiger eyeing his meal. Logan sauntered in with the same look, he smiled down and said. "You deserve a good fucking and a milking. Dillon get her stripped!"

He stripped all her clothing piece by piece until she was naked. Logan stood before her nude his large cock already semi hard. He pressed the head against her lips she opened her mouth licking it, he pressed forward into her as she began to suck, using her tongue on the sensitive underside stimulating him. Rocking his hips he fed more of his long cock into her mouth coming to the back of her throat, she gagged slightly he ignored her reflex feeding more till she had the whole of him down her throat, his balls hanging from her chin. Glancing up at him he stilled for a moment letting her adjust to the fullness, then began rocking back and forth as she licked and sucked making him swell. A groan ripped from his mouth as he blew his salty semen down her throat pumping into her until she had swallowed the last drop. Holding her mouth in an O shape she licked him clean as he withdrew. "Nice sucking Amiela, now you horny little mare we are going to stuff you full and suck your tits when you cum to stimulate your milk flow."

Logan ordered her to the middle of the bed where they cuffed her face down, she found enough slack in the chains to move up onto her hands and knees when ordered. Dillon stuck three long fingers inside her cunt finding her wet. Showing them to Logan he nodded, Logan took the stimulant cream coating her asshole then applied it to his cock. Amiela began to writhe and moan in her chains the effect of the stimulant obvious. Logan poised the large pink head of his cock to her rosette and with a solid push he was thru the tight ring of muscles sinking his cock into her to the hilt. Dillon waited for Logan to sit her back elevating her pussy to receive his long wide cock. Her legs spread wide over his massive thighs opening her pussy lips ready for Dillon to drive deep into her body. One swift thrust he hit her cervix which flowered open enough for his cock to plow thru into her womb. Logan put his finger on her exposed clit rubbing in circles with enough pressure for her clit ring to stimulate from the bottom side. Amiela was stuffed full to overflowing becoming fuller as Dillon moved into her in hard pounding thrusts. She could feel her orgasm tingle to life setting her body on fire before it exploded into a myriad of colours before her eyes, making her scream in ecstasy. With a tit in each hand they latched onto her nipples sucking strongly until her milk gushed into their mouths. As the next orgasm hit her all they had to do was hold her nipples and swallow as the milk poured out of her large teats. On she went from one strong orgasm to the next as Dillon ravaged her cunt mercilessly wringing every ounce of passion out of her till she blacked out. Depleted they withdrew from her body leaving her to come to on her own. They went and showered and dressed coming back with a short red dress that would barely cover anything she had to offer complimented with a pair of red shiny heels.

When they entered the playroom it was empty, Dillon checked the bathroom and found Amiela soaking in the oversize bathtub with the jets turned on churning the water this way and that. She had her eyes closed as though she were sleeping or perhaps relaxing.

"Hey honey, how do you feel?"

Opening her eyes she smiled. "Pretty good considering how thoroughly you took me."

Dillon smiled back thinking how beautiful she was with her guard gone getting thoroughly fucked and milked.

There was going to be a lot more of that in the weeks to come.

"Are you done? Logan and I have a surprise for you."

"Can you hand me that towel over there? I'm ready to get out now."

Handing her the towel he noticed her breasts were back to normal size even after they had milked her hmm he wondered how much milk she would produce tonight at milking time.

Drying her body to a rosy glow Dillon came up behind her rubbing cream into her skin, she needed the stimulant every day now till the party to keep her hot and horny. A few test runs in between were in order as well. Wrapping the towel around her breasts she walked into the playroom with Dillon following close behind.

Logan smiled holding the red dress up for her inspection.

"Oh its lovely, thank you I love it."

Logan helped her into the free flowing confection doing up the clips in back then taking the two halter pieces smoothing them over her breasts and clipping them together. The dress fell freely from under her breasts to the tops of her thighs. He placed the three inch heels on her feet, admiring their slutty little mare.

"Wow you look fantastic!" He complimented her as she looked in the mirror thinking it was a bit short, turning she found it just covered her bare ass.

"I agree, you might need these too." Dillon said handing her a pair of red thong panties. She took them and slipped them on the silk triangle only covering her hairless mound, the thong ran between her pussy lips applying pressure to her clit. Dillon looked for signs of arousal and seeing her flush and fidget slightly told him the stimulant impregnated silk worked.

Logan wanted to show her off to everyone on the ranch.

"Shall we go find some drinks?" He said holding his arm out to Amiela.

They made their way to the kitchen bar area, Dillon reached in the fridge and pulled out a bottle of pinot she liked motioning to her she nodded sitting on a stool at the breakfast bar. Placing the wine by her hand he poured one for himself Logan had opted for red his particular favorite.

"Now that we're all here together let me say we didn't think we were out of line by omitting to tell you about the hormones, since you had a problem with that and other things we will be upfront with you from now on ok."

Amiela nodded letting him continue. "Tonight we have a few of the ranch personnel coming for drinks to get to know you, now before you rush off to get changed you are perfect the way you are, and we would like you to leave your dress as is. If you insist on changing your only other choice that we will accept is a long transparent negligee. Which will it be?"

"I'll wear this, if you're sure its not to dressy." Amiela replied in a soft calm voice.

"Its perfect as I said."

So I wore the red dress to the impromptu party, meeting Slim who I knew a little and Ross who was the ranch's head mechanic and a dozen others whose names eluded me after saying hello. They all watched me in my very short red dress with lustful hungry eyes as I made the rounds in the living room chatting with one man or another. Several times I found someone brushing by me touching my ass or my breasts making it seem accidental. I had the feeling that it was orchestrated when I was moved around the room needing to meet a man and having to squeeze between two or more men to reach the intended recipient.

I kept wondering if they all knew of my forced lactation or perhaps they just liked well endowed women. One thing was for sure the amount of testosterone in the room made me hot and very horny, my pussy kept clenching trying to milk my thong. I could have taken any two or three of them somewhere private and fucked their brains out. The thought that kept me going was my milking was coming soon so I coped with my arousal as they started to leave it became more difficult to suppress my urges to cum, but I did it.

My breasts were painful needing to be expressed and when I couldn't take any more I walked up to Dillon who put his arm around my waist patting my ass in front of Slim and Ross. I whispered in his ear hoping they wouldn't hear. "I need to be milked now, can we excuse ourselves so I can get some relief?"

"Sure baby, no problem."

Excusing ourselves from our guests we made our way across the living room through the kitchen to the sunroom where Dillon kept the milking machine in the large walk-in closet. I noticed crossing the threshold the large room was furnished with a sofa, love seat, and armchairs. Tables sat at the sides of every available seat. "Dillon why is all this furniture in here? Last time there was nothing but the view."

"We thought we may start using this more since you seem to like it so much." He replied as he placed the milking machine to face the window, the sun was just starting to set. Red and gold beams shimmered off it painting the land and mountains in a rosy hue. Un hooking her dress she stepped out of it, lowering her panties she took them off setting everything aside on the nearest chair. She went to the machine sinking gratefully onto the seat as Dillon strapped her wrists and ankles down into position admiring her nude pussy nicely on display, fingering it lightly brought a passionate moan out of Amiela making him smile taking note of her creamy wet pussy. The stimulant worked better than he had imagined it would being absorbed by her pussy made her ready for anything. He had impregnated six pairs of her new panties with it, maybe he should do more only leaving her without it every so often.

Attaching the cups to her extended nipples he turned the milker on, she orgasmed  screaming out her pleasure. Flipping the switch for the dildo he held her pussy lips open so the head could penetrate her cunt. It slipped inside about three inches he turned the dial and it began pumping gaining depth on each plunge into her slippery vagina. Amiela didn't notice when Slim, Ross and Logan entered the room so far gone into her sensual bliss she could only feel the next stronger orgasm take her to pleasure she had never known.

They admired her curvy body for a few moments watching her lose all sense of self to the bliss she was experiencing. Speaking in hushed tones Slim remarked.

"I would love to fuck and suck the milk from her tits every time she needs relief."

"Maybe you will before long, Dillon and I need to see if she is into that or not."

Satisfied Slim turned his attention to the erotic sight of Amiela clearly loving her new cock and hoped she would be ok with multiple partners.

~~~~

## Chapter Three Coming Changes

Amiela awoke with a start finding herself alone with full breasts that were edging toward painful. Crawling out of bed her feet hit the floor as memories from last night hit her brain, the party where she seemed to be the entrée. Those gave her delicious little thrills to think all those men would want her. And the milking was as mind blowing as it had been before only better some how. She mulled that over on her way to the shower turning it on and stepping inside to ten different heads giving her pleasure. She let a giggle slip through her lips. Soaping up she found her nipples were tender as well as her clit. Pain shot through her breasts when the water hit them hurrying her to finish so she could relieve them. Emerging from the bathroom she found a short silk wrap in the closet donning it as she went to the kitchen looking for one of her guys to express her milk. The sapphire blue she loved, thank you personal shopper she thought. Entering the kitchen she found only Slim making breakfast.

"Good morning Amiela, did you sleep ok last night?" He asked giving her a sexy wolfish look.

"Yes, like a log thank you. Do you know where Dillon or Logan might be?"

"They had an emergency early this morning with one of the horses, they should be back before long. Something you need them for?" He asked looking like he could devour her on the spot. Great now what do I do? My milk has to come out now, I can't take any more. She thought as she fidgeted with the pain and pressure in her tits. Not to mention she was horny, feeling a slickness on her inner thighs as her pussy clenched and drooled.

"Well its just, well my breasts need to be expressed and could you help me maybe get hooked up to the machine so I can get some relief." Amiela was red faced by the time she said it, she was embarrassed, mortified, the works.

Slim looked at her with a broad smile on his face. "Sure I would be happy to help." He replied coming toward her at a leisurely pace, like he was approaching a skittish horse. Placing his hand on her shoulder he touched the side of her breast with the other. Through the silk of her wrap he felt the rock hardness of her tit.

"You do need to be milked alright." He said brushing the wrap aside to bare her breast, taking the extended nipple in his mouth he sucked hard making her wince till it was replaced by pleasure of having release. Latching on to her other nipple she orgasmed at the first strong pull of his mouth.

"Looks like you need more than just milking, I can oblige you there too if you like?"

Amiela was past the point of caring how she got relief as long as she did, now. "Thanks that would be great."

"Ok, lets get you milked." He said smiling leading her into the sun room. She sat on the milking seat with pleasure blossoming in her entire being.

Taking her hand he had her stand up, took her wrap off attached the nipple cups then instructed her to bend over and put her hands on the arms of the milking stool. He turned it on, undressing as he watched the milk dribble down the tubes.

"Ok baby I'm going to fuck you from behind like the good little filly that you are." That said he eased his long thick cock inside her bottoming out at her cervix.

Nudging it with the head he realized it was opening enough that the tip of his cock got inside, continuing he gave a couple more thrusts and he was through into her womb. Her milk was filling the tubes to capacity as he thrust back and forth. She orgasmed again and again he lost count, with her cunt squeezing him hard he came and came slumping forward onto her back bracing himself on the arms of the chair. Coming around after the best sex of his life he noticed the flow had diminished to a fine trickle. He took the cups off her breasts turning the machine off. Helping her to a nearby armchair he knelt in front of her spread thighs latching on to her perky peg and stripped first one breast than the other dry.

After a while Amiela became fully aware of being dressed in her short wrap by Slim.

"Thank you I feel much better now, what's for breakfast?"

"The works, come I will get you squared away."

Now that her immediate needs were taken care of she was starving.

Seating herself Slim set a large plate of food in front of her and she began with a strip of bacon munching happily. Thinking of her encounter with Slim, she wondered how Logan and Dillon would take the news that she had fucked him stupid and vice versa. Time to worry about that when she told them. Logan walked into the kitchen halfway through Amiela's breakfast looking content. Glancing across the room she caught his satisfied grin knowing everything this morning went well disaster averted.

"Good morning Amiela, I trust everything went well in our absence." Logan joined her at the table bending down to give her a toe curling kiss.

"Yes it was fine." Amiela lowered her eyes feeling slightly guilty over the fact her actions with Slim were not something she was looking forward to telling them.

"Great I knew Slim could handle it." Logan remarked casually sitting down as Slim put a plate loaded with food in front of him. Dillon came in going straight to Amiela bent down and gave her a mind numbing kiss that made her pussy clench with need. 'She thought I need a cock now, what is this need I have all the time to be screwed senseless.'

Finishing her breakfast Amiela excused herself  intent on grabbing a shower no longer wanting to smell sex on herself.

Standing under the sensual spray all her nerve endings came to screaming life making her desperate for release. Fingering her slick pussy she stroked in and out while circling her clit with her finger bringing on a gasping orgasm leaving her sated as she finished up not minding she no longer had to shave anything to be soft and silky. Stepping out she took a towel off the warming rack drying every inch with care. Brushing out her long hair she clipped it up in a messy ponytail to dry while she applied moisturizer to her body enjoying the feel of her firm silky skin under her fingertips. Turning to enter the bedroom she caught the hint of a shadow moving about, peeking around the door she saw Dillon holding a black lacy negligee inspecting it's construction.

"Hi, what's up?"

"We have to put the nipple stretchers on you to lengthen your nipples a bit more." He replied so easily like it was a foregone conclusion that this was the way it would be.

I caved nodding my head in agreement, just the thought of having his hands on my breasts turned me on fiercely.

"Lay down on the bed and I'll attach the pump." His face looked thunderous accepting no argument that I could give even if I could have thought of one. Doing as I was told I climbed onto the bed getting comfortable lying on my back. Dillon took my left hand cuffing it gently then moving to my right side he repeated the process. My ankles came next spreading my legs wide. Satisfied I was held securely he climbed on the bed positioned to my left. Fingering my nipple he squeezed until it hardened.

"Nice its an inch long and plump as a berry. Won't be long till you have nice long pegs to suck." He said smiling down placing the clear acrylic tube over my nipple. It was some four inches long held by light suction. This was the first time I had seen the machine, there were three vials attached to clear plastic tubing that lead to a small black box holding several dials.

"Nice, now this little tube here is for your clit, I'm going to pull it out more stretch it so it's bigger. By the time I'm finished it will look like a small cherry sitting at the top of your pussy folds."

I didn't reply as none was required he was doing it whether I liked it or not and I did like it. Stimulating my clit he attached the pump just as it peeked out. He turned the machine on by twisting a dial and my nipples and clit were sucked halfway up the vials. Thank god the one on my clit was only a couple of inches long. It felt good though, tingled a bit made me wet between my thighs. As my pussy clenched he rubbed a dildo up and down my slit seeking entrance pushing it into my body a bit at a time, it felt huge as it stretched my inner walls filling me up beyond anything I had taken inside me thus far. Fully seating it he turned it on via a remote control, inspecting my nipples and clit inside the vials he turned the vacuum pump off removing the tubes setting them on the night table beside the control box leaving the vials attached to my body. "The vials stay on this morning then we'll see how much progress we made. How do you feel?"

Concentrating was difficult as I was nearing orgasm but some how I answered. "Fine ahhhhhhhh gonna cum Mmmm.". He turned the dildo up so it pumped inside me sending me over the edge in a massive screaming orgasm. I vaguely felt him remove it going into the bathroom he came back to me a few minutes later opening the drawer beside the bed he removed a box.

"I have something for you which we will put on this afternoon." Opening it he showed me three intricately carved gold rings about a quarter of an inch wide and three inches in diameter. All had thick closure bars on them with a large diamond the size if a robin egg suspended in the centre of each.

"These are new additions for your nipples and clit, do you like them?"

"Their lovely thank you." I wasn't sure about the size and how I would wear them under my clothes unseen but then I thought maybe the point was for them to be seen.

Holding his hand out to  he indicated for me to get up. I stood on the floor feeling a bit weak in the knees, Dillon assisted moving forward till I stood in front of the closet where the negligee was hanging. Taking it off the hanger he held it out while I put my arms in the long sleeves, he came around in front of me loosely tying the two ribbons one at my sternum the other a couple of inches lower.

"Lets go have coffee with Logan then after lunch we can take the stretchers off and get you outfitted in your new jewelry."

"Ok coffee sounds good."

We walked out of the bedroom down the long hall to the stairs where I paused to take a breath. The feeling of the vial between my legs was working my clit making my pussy clench with every step. At this rate I would cum again before I made it too the kitchen.

"Horny again Amiela, are you ready to cum?" Dillon asked with a very satisfied look on his face.

"Yes I panted."

"Good then it's doing its job of making your clit more sensitive. Bringing it out to play if you will. Let's go Logan is waiting." He gave me his arm for support as we descended the stairs into the living room.

Logan came to meet us at the bottom. He wore a knowledgeable look making me nervous bringing back my milking sex with Slim. Assisting me onto the sofa Logan sat in the armchair to my left pouring coffee into mugs fixing it the way we all liked it just black. Handing me the cup he asked "So we're you alright with Slim helping with your milking this morning?"

"Ummm yes it was fine."

"Good he loved fucking and milking you too, so much so that he is anticipating the next time. Are you agreeable to having him again?"

"Yes if neither of you are around to help me."

Logan sat back sipping his coffee considering her answer. Dillon reflected on her statement knowing neither of them were satisfied with her response, it seemed she would only take a chance on something new if her comfort zone were gone and she had no other choice. Glancing over to Logan he saw the same conclusion set in his face, so their little Amiela would be given no choices other than what they chose for her. However on the surface it would look like she made the decision.

"Alright I can live with that honey, we both want only what is best for you to experience.

How do you like the expanders?"

"Fine as long as I'm not moving about, otherwise not so much."

Logan could see lust in her eyes and her little squirming told him she was very horny and that was ok by him.

"I think we should go have lunch then we can outfit you with your new gifts." Logan rose moving to help Amiela, once she was standing he picked her up and carried his precious bundle into the kitchen sitting her down on the chair that was now hers positioned between them.

Slim was busy making a chicken salad on rye bread and tending his simmering soup when they arrived. He turned at their entry having eyes only for Amiela in her black lace negligee which he agreed set off all her assets to perfection. Large round breasts and a pussy any man would have wet dreams about.

"Hey lunch almost ready?" Dillon asked appreciating the wolfish look his woman was getting.

"Yep all done." Slim returned bringing the soup to the table not taking his eyes off her. He hoped she had consented to be on loan to him sometimes because he sure enjoyed his morning's work with her.

Setting the vegetable soup down in front of everyone he saved Amiela's till last lingering a moment longer than necessary placing it, brushing the slope of her breast and shoulder as he proceeded to get the sandwiches. They noticed a shiver run through her body from his touch, smiles lighted all around.

During the meal Amiela squirmed and moved trying to make herself comfortable with the vials attached to her nipples and clit but all she managed was to drive her unruly body into a sexual frenzy. Nearing the end she stated "Dillon these have to come off now! I can't take any more please." Shaking she touched his arm begging to be released.

Dillon looked from her imploring eyes to her hand on his arm trying to be still but failing.

"Alright lets go you have hit your outside limit, best to get it done now. Are you coming Logan?"

"Wouldn't miss it." He returned with a grin.

Assisting Amiela one on each side they made their way to the ER where this procedure would be completed.

Strapping her hands above her head Logan tethered each ankle to either side of the table so her legs were spread wide. Placing a small roll pillow under her brought her hips up placing her clit on display.

Dillon released the vacuum on the vials taking them off producing a gasping moan from Amiela.

"Are you alright baby?" Not really expecting an answer as worked up as she was. Inspecting her nipples he noticed they were a quarter of an inch longer and staying hard standing out from her areola. Her clit had done much better with the procedure standing proudly like a small ripe cherry. Laving it with his tongue sent her into a screaming orgasm. While she was writhing on the table he retrieved the tray of supplies he would need.

Standing between her spread thighs he admired how perfect she was, a thrill going through him as he was about to add another ring to her clit. Applying the anesthesia to her clitoris he then applied it to each of her nipples. Taking the hot piercing wand he gently but firmly made a hole large enough for the very course ring to slide through. He had decided on the wand after her last piercings took longer than normal to heal.

Sliding the bar on the ring into her clit he clicked it closed then using the unique screwdriver he had made he locked it shut. This ring was much larger and also had a two carat diamond suspended from it. She would feel all her new rings more now given the weight of the stones.

Moving on to her breasts he placed the wand behind her previous piercing making two holes in quick succession. Sliding the bar thru one breast he locked it and then the other. The new rings would keep her longer nipples harder and also stimulate her. More was to be done with the length but for now it was enough.

Logan took the straps off and helped her down from the exam table walking to the mirror he asked.

"So what do you think of your new rings?" Amiela looked at herself liking the new look.

"I love them thank you both."

This pleased them and Dillon knew in that instant that he loved her and finally his destiny was looking back at him through the mirror.

Coming Home Series News

Coming Home Logan's Wish Book one

Coming Home Dillon's Destiny Book two

Coming next in the series Coming Home Amiela's Submission Book three

# Coming Home
Amiela's Submission
Author:Adeline Moore
Copyright 2014 Adeline Moore

ISBN:978-0-9919593-5-8
This book is intended for those of you over 18. Mature Content.

Dedication
Anything worth having is worthy of your thought.

## Coming Trials

Amiela looked at her reflection in the mirror admiring her new rings, they are so awesome she thought smiling to herself, this was another dream she had and one more was fulfilled thanks to Dillon and Logan. Having them had been a fantasy she never would have accomplished on her own. She simply didn't have the guts to go thru with it even though she had made the appointments then canceled when she chickened out. They knew what she wanted before she voiced anything even her secret wish to lactate without having a baby, although it would have been nice if they had consulted her first but in hindsight she knew this was the best way. As for being sexually free she knew she wasn't there yet, perhaps one day soon.

"So from that smile on your face we take it that you like them?" Logan asked glancing from the rings to her face marveling at how beautiful she was.

"Yes I love them, I have wished for these for a very long time, I just couldn't bring myself to getting them done." Amiela felt herself blushing at the admission.

"You can go and get dressed if you like just be careful not to wear anything restrictive as it will irritate the new piercings. Something loose and flowing for the next week should do it." Dillon smiled as Amiela put on her robe and left them.

Climbing the stairs she noticed the ring hanging from her clit as she moved, it moved with her causing twinges in her pussy via her clit. The weight would take some time to get used to. Her longer nipples stood erect poking through the silk robe, the outline of her rings apparent for everyone to see. Now this will definitely take time to become accustomed to. She had always been as bit shy and self conscious of her body, being teased as a teenager by her two older brothers for being chubby and then as her growth accelerated it was for being skinny, everything eventually settled into a well shaped package in her twenties. She had a nice figure and men seemed to enjoy watching her, now with her double D breasts she felt a bit top heavy but when she looked in the mirror she saw a lush body, long legs, flat tummy, tiny waist everything seemed so much more pronounced, feeling like she was looking at someone else. Turning from her reflection she opened her closet, walking inside touching the numerous outfits she owned feeling their varied textures from silky to soft and comforting. Deciding on a blue and green floral top with just the right amount of flow to camouflage her larger set of rings and the plunging cowl neckline showed just enough cleavage, she turned to the other side of the closet flicking through skirts hoping to find a modest length she could sit comfortably in. After twenty minutes all she found was one that came to mid thigh, at least the navy blue would help, it also went nicely with the sleeveless top. Slipping it over her head she stepped into the skirt zipping it, surveying her reflection in the standing mirror, she liked it, even the skirt which was shorter than she normally wore looked good showing a large amount of leg which made her feel sexy. Sliding her feet into a pair of blue and green beaded heels she felt she was ready for whatever her day had in store.

Leaving the bedroom she made her way to the office anticipating doing some work on her wolf transplant project before lunch. All the government paperwork needed to be filed with the appropriate departments so the final approvals were granted in time for next spring, then the real work would begin. Between now and then she had lots of time to see exactly where her relationship with Logan and Dillon was going. Immersed in red tape she didn't know Dillon was standing in the office door speaking to her until he raised his voice asking.

"Are you coming for lunch, its ready?"

Jerking her head up she almost made a mess of the form she was filling out.

"Um yes I'm coming."

Rising to her feet she walked around the desk receiving an appreciative whistle for her trouble. Blushing she took the arm Dillon offered slipping hers in the crook of his elbow. More whistles from Logan, Slim and Ross greeted her as they entered the kitchen.

"You look stunning Amiela!" Logan exclaimed coming over and giving her a bone melting kiss.

"Thank you." She replied seating herself on the chair Logan pulled out for her. Lunch was a simple spinach salad with ham and beef tossed together with some goat's cheese and a delicious mandarin orange dressing. Picking up her glass she took a sip and discovered a crisp white wine with a pear finish that complimented the food.

"How did your work go this morning Amiela?" Logan asked breaking the silence surrounding the table.

"Pretty good, I got a decent start on the red tape your government requires for the transplant. I should have the final approvals in six months, plenty of time before we head into the final phase in the spring when my team arrives."

Squirming on the hard wooden seat everyone at the table noticed making her blush profusely but made no comment to her discomfort. She tried to find an acceptable position so her clit ring would stop stimulating her already overheated pussy. For sure she thought she would have a wet spot on her skirt when she finally stood. Conversation flowed around her as her orgasm mounted coming ever closer to exploding like four of July fireworks. Taking hold of the table's edge she attempted to stem the flow but only managed by shifting slightly to bring it to fruition. Moaning then screaming out her pleasure in front of the four men who watched her like hungry wolves with bulges in their jeans and carnal lust in their eyes. Coming down after flying into the heavens Amiela looked around finding all eyes on her making her turn ten shades of red in quick succession.

"Excuse me." She said softly embarrassed to the roots of her hair, mortified beyond anything she had ever experienced before. Making her way to her bedroom on shaky legs she collapsed on the bed, tears snaking down her face in jagged rivulets. She knew she was feeling sorry for herself and that did not help to dry her tears, the guys probably loved seeing her orgasm at lunch but she wasn't comfortable with it, it made her feel slutty and as of yet she hadn't embraced that fully. Slipping off her shoes first one then the other they made a soft thump on the thick carpet as they hit the floor. Curling in a ball she poured her tears into the pillow until she fell asleep exhausted from her emotional storm.

Dillon sauntered in several hours later not expecting to find her curled in a tight ball with tear stains on her face, whimpering slightly in her sleep. He figured when she left at lunch she needed a little time to herself so they had let her be to come to terms with her display. Now he wondered if they hadn't screwed up with her again, she obviously needed one of them to comfort her and reassure her that her orgasm had been fine and they all had very much enjoyed seeing her passion. But how did she interpret it? Covering her with a throw he left the bedroom heading to the kitchen to talk to Logan who was making dinner.

"Where's Amiela?" Was the first question out of his mouth when Dillon entered the room.

"Sleeping. It seems today was pretty hard on her, she was crying for quite awhile after she left at lunch judging from the tear stains and red rimmed eyes. I decided to let her be."

Logan listened and agreed with Dillon, they could always take up a tray later if she chose not to come down for dinner. Hell if she needed space they could always sleep in their old bedrooms for a night or two.

"So what you're saying is, she was upset by her orgasming at lunch. Maybe she just needs some time and space to come to terms with it."

"No, I think she needs reassurance and caring. More time away from us isn't going to make her feel any better, I think she might run again if we don't show her it was wonderful seeing her lost in her pleasure. I know Ross and Slim were ecstatic she allowed them to see her like that, they've been talking about it all afternoon."

Logan listened wondering if Dillon wasn't right, perhaps they needed to show her how wonderful everything was now that she had moved in. Rethinking dinner he packaged the meat and vegetables into containers and stowed them in the refrigerator. Rummaging through the sub zero freezer he found some homemade chicken soup and cheese biscuits he knew Amiela loved, the chocolate caramel nut tart would do nicely in cheering her up as well. Popping the soup in the microwave to thaw he turned to Dillon standing by the bar with a glass and a bottle of scotch.

"Care for a drink?"

"Good idea might take the edge off. I thought we could take a tray up and spent the night helping Amiela see that freedom to be who she was meant to be, is a very good thing."

Taking the tray they made their way to the master bedroom to find Amiela exactly where Dillon had left her curled up in a fetal position covered with the throw, her eyes still red around the edges although the puffiness had disappeared. Sensing someone in the room woke her with a start, sitting up wiping the hair away from her face she smiled still groggy from her long sleep. Feeling dampness on her chest she knew from the chill on her breasts that she was leaking milk although she wasn't hurting yet but knew she would be soon.

Noticing the milk stain on her blouse Logan set the tray down on the night table sitting beside her on the bed he caressed her cheek with his palm. "You need to be milked sweetie, are you feeling better?"

"Some what, I'm still mortified orgasming at lunch like that, I can't believe my new rings stimulate me so much. God they must think I'm an insatiable slut."

"Honey they loved it, thought in fact it was the sexiest thing they have seen in a long time." Dillon replied smiling conveying it was wonderful.

Taking this in the fashion it was meant she felt better. She wasn't ready to repeat the act any time soon but it gave her a new found confidence that perhaps when it happened she could simply move forward without destroying herself emotionally.

"I need to get out of these clothes and grab a shower, I'm sticky from leaking milk, I feel very grubby anyone care to join me?" With that she had both of them smiling.  Logan helped her from the bed as Dillon went off to start the shower to make it perfect for them. Disposing of her clothes with a lot of kissing and touching she was ready to explode before she made it to the bathroom.

Picking her up she wrapped her legs around his naked waist as he carried her into the massive multi nozzle shower.  Water rained down and around them in a warm steamy torrent.  Dillon watched from his seat in the corner as Logan positioned his cock at her opening and thrust up into her slick pussy.  With a moan she came voicing her pleasure in punctuated grunts as Logan pounded into her.  Her nipples let a stream of creamy milk go washing away down the drain.

Dillon thought they should've milked her before showering then thought better of it as she would make more, the customers wouldn't be deprived, everyone was happy with the situation. Joining them Dillon took a nipple in his mouth sucking greedily sending Amiela into an orgasm that streamed creamy milk into his mouth, he never tired of milking her breasts letting himself be drawn in to her pleasure feeling as though it was his.  As her milk dwindled to a single drop he let go of her nipple, switching sides to latch onto her other long nipple.  The stretching and the new rings had worked wonders her nipples were a inch and three quarters perfect for his lips to suck on or hold in his mouth as her milk streamed out.  Amiela's moans spurred Dillon's semi hard erection to blossom into a full hard on that stood proudly, its length reaching his belly button.  Taking it in hand she worked him until his groans filled the shower drowning out hers and Logan's.

Feeling his ejaculation coming he aimed his penis at the juncture of her thighs where her and Logan were joined releasing his cum between them covering her bare pussy and his brother's cock which spurred them on to completion.

Letting go of her legs Amiela slide down Logan's wet front till her feet touched the floor, using his shoulders for balance until she could support her own weight even though her legs felt weak and wobbly from the session she had been gifted. Dillon turned to her with a puff and shower gel then went to work cleansing her body with the vanilla apricot gel with added moisture he had ordered from a friend who made holistic soaps. In turn she returned the favor enjoying ever second, her equilibrium restored. Stepping out they both dried her body then rubbed moisturizer onto every square inch of her body.

Logan took the silk robe he had chosen in a dark midnight blue which brought the dark lights out in her eyes making them smoldering. He liked her that way sexy, alluring with a come fuck me look. If she could get past her hangups about nudity and sex they would have everything they had ever wanted in a wife. Watching was his and Dillon's thing they loved it and neither could see going without it. Taking Amiela's hand he tugged until she followed him into the bedroom seating her in the sofa in front of the fireplace.

"We need to talk about what happened at lunch, more specifically your reaction. We all loved seeing you cum, it was so free, and you have never been more beautiful than in those moments." Leaving it for the time being he watched her seeing shame, guilt, and embarrassment but underneath he saw gratification, courage, and happiness.

Amiela was taken aback by his comment not sure what to say now that her stress over the coming in public was behind her, if she told the truth she secretly loved being watched by four horny men, it gave her a power she never knew she possessed. Phrasing her words carefully she replied. "It upset me at the time but now it doesn't feel bad, it actually feels pretty good to know I can turn other men on besides you and Dillon."

Logan beamed a megawatt smile "Great! I knew you would come into it eventually. So would you be ok with fucking other men while we watched?"

"You would be cool with that, I mean most men wouldn't want their woman whoring herself."

"I am happy you are considering being our hot wife. We both love to watch you being fucked by other men, and milked too. So what do you say we give you an opportunity to whore yourself out on a larger scale than anything you've done before."

"What exactly are you proposing?" Amiela looked in his eyes to see if he were serious.

"Well for starters a small get together of twenty of our closest friends who know that we watch and either do it themselves or understand the need. All of which are breastmilk connoisseurs especially yours since they have been supplied by you for several weeks now. They would all like the opportunity to drink from your nipples and have sex with you, are you going to be alright with that many men seeing and hearing you cum?"

Amiela sat there stunned by his admission thinking would that be ok, could she do it?

"I don't know part of me thinks I could but the other part is terrified of the thought."

"How did you feel when Slim milked and fucked you?"

"It was good, I needed to be milked desperately that morning and when he offered I couldn't say no. I enjoyed being with him and he gave me some really fantastic orgasms."

"Ok, will you try this for yourself first and then for us? We want you to be free to have sex with whomever you wish, the only condition is Dillon and I watch."

"I will try but no promises on the outcome."

"I understand, you do know that no harm will come to you, we will be with you and these men are only into the thrill and gratification of pleasing a woman on every level till she melts with pleasure. You will feel extraordinary afterward." Logan smiled taking away the tension replacing it with hot need.

"Now it's time you eat, there is more ahead for you tonight." Wrapping his fingers around mine he led me down to the kitchen where Dillon was busy warming something on the stove, glancing at the island there were two glasses of wine one red one white. Logan took the white handing it over to me.

"Thank you." I spoke softly a smile transformed Logan's stern face into a gentle softness.

"Amiela has consented to having the party. Next weekend is a long holiday how about then, will that give you enough time to get everything together?" Logan asked Dillon.

"Ya should be, a little extra may have to be given but I can manage it. You do know there are a lot of men who want to get to know you right?"

"Logan mentioned twenty or are there more than that coming?"

"Might be more but they will all be given a day of the weekend with you so no more than ten a day over the five day weekend. They will arrive on Thursday and leave on tuesday. All the replies will be in by this weekend so I will know more then. Are you feeling alright with this?" Dillon asked a frown etching his strong handsome face.

"I will try, no promises to the outcome but it will be nice to meet your friends." Dillon gave Logan a look Amiela couldn't decipher so passed it off looking toward the stove. Dillon poured the soup into bowls setting them on the table with the biscuits and dessert. Amiela started to feel full so she left her soup and half eaten biscuit pushing them aside in favor of her wine.

"Not hungry?" Dillon asked concern written in his expression.

"No, I don't have much of an appetite tonight. It's just the stress from today, nothing to worry about." She passed it off lightly hoping he would drop the subject.

"Perhaps you won't be strung out about appearing sexually after you have a taste of it. You could embrace today and go on a much stronger person for the experience."

Saying nothing in return she excused herself heading out of the room with her glass and the bottle of wine determined to lock herself in the bathroom, have a bath and drink till the bottle was empty and perhaps going for round two.

Dillon looked at Logan with a fuck me on his face. "I wonder if I overstepped with that!"

"Well no use worrying about it now, if anything it will give her something to think on and maybe come to the conclusion we all have, a woman is a very sexual being and it just takes the right men and a bit of persuasion to bring out the whore we love seeing. We gave her a wardrobe full of sexy things, we have her lactating, the next step is the party where she will definitely be the star."

"You're right given that she goes through with letting everyone or at least most screw her brains out. I'll start giving her a double dose of the stimulant Matt sent, so by next weekend she will be wanting to have sex with everyone.  Of course she will think it's just her reacting naturally to the situation and we will support that idea. Her body lotion has it in it too so we're covered."

Logan rose from the table carrying the dishes from dinner. "Good all will be as we planned then." He loaded the dishes in the dishwasher then grabbed the bottle of red wine refilling his glass. With a nod Dillon followed Logan out of the kitchen with the bottle of body oil his friend had sent intent on giving Amiela a massage and a good screwing. The properties in the oil and body lotion as well as her oral dose would build up slowly in her system over the next week so by thursday night she would be very horny. All her milk buyers had jumped at the chance to come and suck direct and fuck her, should be an interesting long weekend.

Logan entered the massive bedroom finding no Amiela and the bathroom door closed. Hmm looks like she's having a bath, turning the knob produced nothing, its locked even more interesting she must be mad if she thinks a locked door will stop him from getting to her. Reaching up he feels the key sitting on the wide moulding above his head, taking it in his finger and thumb he inserts the key in the lock freeing the door which swings open with a nudge hitting the stop making a loud thud. Amiela's eyes spring open from her meditation landing on Logan in the doorway with Dillon behind looking over his shoulder eating her up with his sparkling blue eyes.

"Its time for your massage come out of the bath and lie on the table, Dillon is an expert with a bit of oil!" Logan commands leaving no doubt refusal is not an option. Moving into the giant spacious bathroom he opens the cabinet takes out a fluffy white towel meeting her beside the tub he goes to work drying her off. 'When did I start doing as he tells me she wonders, I automatically did as he commanded without a thought to refusing, maybe the wine hit me harder than I..... No its not that this is all me, this makes me feel good to have no choice, no thought about consequences, just do as I am bid. There is a great freedom in it, bliss almost.'

"Ok now go lay face down on the table, Dillon is waiting for you." He gave her a smack on the butt on her way past him, it stung hot giving her pussy a jolt of moisture, looking over her shoulder he shrugged and winked making her think he had wanted to do that for awhile.

Seeing his hand print turning red on her right cheek thrilled him and made him damned hard. He enjoyed spanking a woman occasionally if she were into it and it looked like Amiela was. Reaching the massage table Dillon had set up by the large windows facing over the drive and the ranch buildings she wondered if anyone was out there looking in, they would get a perfect view of her naked body standing and lying on the table while Dillon massaged her. Getting into position face down on the table she relaxed while Dylan's hands went to kneading out all the knots her stress had produced recently. His hands were magic sending her into a semi conscious state of bliss, sending warm tingles to her breasts and pussy all at the same time. Amiela's concerns wafted away replaced by the need to be touched more intimately, reading her body Dillon knew what she wanted, reaching her buttocks in his ministrations he slid two oiled fingers into her anal passage working them around loosening her sphincter muscles then added a third working her out further, satisfied he withdrew wiped his hands on a wet towel and proceeded down her leg to her foot. Adding more oil he transferred his attention to her opposite foot working the muscles into a relaxed state. He knew he had her on a knife's edge and fully intended keeping her there until he deemed it time to make her cum. He loved this power he had over her, she was agreeing more often to their proposals and hopefully this would continue through the party they had been planning for her from the beginning of their relationship, for him and Logan too there was an undeniable need to see her being fucked by other men. Reaching her pussy he toyed with her lips for a moment then plunged four oiled fingers inside her vagina making her moan raising her ass off the table giving him more access.

"Hold that pose for a bit. It's the perfect time...." Dillon commanded then trailed off saying what was on his mind, no point in alarming her with his intentions.  Reaching under the table he opened a drawer taking out the necessary items then closed it silently. Taking a small dildo between his fingers he inserted it gradually up her rectum seating itself as her anal ring squeezed around in the groove provided ensuring it stayed in place. This particular device had a acrylic tube in its centre, he took the syringe placing it on the tube and pushed the plunger dispensing its contents inside. Taking a larger dildo of the same design he pushed it up her vagina working it in and out fucking her bumping up against her cervix to Amiela's moans and squeals of pleasure. Grabbing up a larger syringe he repeated the process emptying its contents into her vagina, working it in and out till he was assured all the liquid had disappeared inside her then he withdrew it leaving her ass stuffed.  That should do nicely he thought to ensure she was horny and promiscuous for the party. Her shyness would be overcome by her sex drive allowing her more freedom.  He continued massaging up her back to her shoulders then motioned for her to turn onto her back.  Settling down she gave a long sigh and closed her eyes.  He massaged her shoulders then the tops of her breasts working his way around each one in a circular motions tweaking her nipple rings to renew her sexual high, her moans indicated her progress. Working down over her ribs and flat stomach he moved her belly button ring making her squirm. Her thighs and pussy beckoned his talented hands as he inched his way down her leg spending time on her feet to stimulate her sex centres. Up her other leg till he arrived at her pussy flicking her clit ring while he stimulated her pleasure nub to bring her on the edge of orgasm once again.  Stopping he buckled a leather cuff around her wrist he retrieved from under the table the continued to cuff her opposite wrist then her ankles assuring she was restrained he walked across the room to a closet he kept supplies in opened the door retrieving the pumps he used to enlarge her nipples and clit, a little more length in her nipples would make them fantastic to suckle and he wanted her clit bigger therefore adding to her overall sex drive ensuring her promiscuity. Returning to Amiela strapped down to the massage table he attached the nipple tubes and the clit tube turned the machine up to maximum suction switched it on and left her to orgasm.

Leaving the bedroom he joined Logan in the living room helping himself to a large measure of scotch.

"So how are things progressing with our slut?" Logan asked eyebrows raised expectantly.

"Doing fine I injected a healthy dose of the aphrodisiac into her anus and vagina where it will absorb into her body doubling its effect daily, she will be the whore we are expecting to see at the party with no reservations about nudity or orgasming or fucking with an audience, she will be thinking about the next cock and the next." Dillon smiled giving the impression this is what he wanted most.

"Great, perhaps after this party she will be fine just going around in see thru robes or nothing at all. I took the liberty of choosing a few outfits for her this week gradually showing more skin as the week progresses.  Get her in the proper frame of mind gradually then hopefully she will think nothing of showing her body off and love it, that's the key.  Where is she now?"

"Still on the table having her nipples and clit extended a little more, probably having one orgasm after another as I left the butt plug in her."

The devious smile on Dillon's face said it all, he loved knowing he caused her to lose her mind with pleasure.  Enjoyed watching her in the throes of passion.

# Coming Business

Amiela awoke the next morning with the sun streaming across the expanse of bed she was laying in trying to get her bearings, the last thing she remembered was Dillon massaging and driving her body crazy with denied pleasure and then all the orgasms she could wish for one after another. Running her hands across her nipples she noticed they were much longer looking down confirmed it, reaching further down she touched her clit, a hard tight ball oh it was larger too and very sensitive. Bringing her hands up to her breasts they were hard and wanting to be expressed but not painful yet. Blowing out a stream of air through her mouth she rolled over to the edge of the bed putting her feet over the side, sitting up she slide off the bed landing on the floor lightly, padding to the closet she grabbed the first robe she came across, a black semi sheer silk with two little ties at her waist. Tying them in a pretty bow she observed her reflection satisfied that none of her body parts showed through the draping layers.
Walking into the kitchen barefoot she heard Dillon say.
"Amiela should be getting up soon, time for her milking."
"Yes, shall we get to it then?" She asked making Dillon and Logan jump at her appearance.
"God you scared me." Dillon replied with a laugh holding his hand over his heart. "Yes we should, after you.". He motioned for her to lead the way admiring the glimpses of skin he was getting through her silk robe.
Logan watched as they adjourned to the sunroom his mother had filled with plants and flowering shrubs, loving everyone in equal measure. Now it was the milking room, a place Amiela loved for the panoramic scene set outside its windows. She said it gave her a calmness to enjoy the pleasures that came with her milk being expressed. Logan had the room wired with closed circuit cameras so they could watch her from any room they chose via their computers or tablets. This little feature would come in handy this weekend as the guests wanted to see her being milked. She

didn't realize but her robe gave a beautiful view of her body through the material, tomorrow it would be a little more visible. Humming, Logan went off to the bedroom he and Dillon shared with Amiela, opening the closet door he felt the silky material of all the lovely wraps and robes they had bought for her. Flipping through the hangers he rearranged them moving the lighter weight ones to the forefront ensuring she would choose one of them, then he moved all her most revealing blouses and shortest skirts to the most desirable spot to be chosen. He proceeded through her entire dressing room moving her garments to his satisfaction. Only the sexiest most revealing were kept front and centre at her fingertips. And all her fuck me shoes were lined up at eye level everything else was moved to the highest shelves where she was unlikely to look given she had to use the ladder to see what was up there. Satisfied, he went to the bedroom flipped on the tablet to see how she was doing with her milking. Watching her slip the flimsy wrap over her shoulders and tie the two ribbons at her waist he admired the cleavage revealed and the shape of her body through the material made very transparent by the light beaming in the windows behind her. One aspect that caught his attention was her smile and the peace and tranquility radiating through the screen. He knew they were on the right path for Amiela to become the woman she was always meant to be.

Amiela made her way to her bedroom on the second floor of the massive home Dillon, Logan and now herself called home. Walking into the room she saw Logan sitting on the sofa with a tablet in his hands, glancing over his shoulder she saw a black screen, Logan was deep in thought starting when she touched his shoulder. Leaning over him she kissed his lips with a searing passion that left him breathless as she drew back.

"I think you enjoyed your milking." Logan stated quirking his lips into a smile.

"Yes I did, but I'm so horny, care to help me satisfy my urges?"

"I would love to but I have some business matters to go over with Dillon so keep that thought for later."Rising he kissed her softly leaving the room. Amiela shot darts at his back with her eyes until he was out of sight.

'Oh damn now I have to take care of myself, damn who would think with two men to have sex with I'm having to get myself off with my dildo!' With that she went to her closet found the drawer where she kept her toys choosing a long thick black one that boasted various speeds.

Walking into the bathroom dildo in hand she set it on the vanity while she turned the nozzles on. Taking off her flimsy robe she tossed it into the laundry hamper, picking up her toy she stepped under the warm water relaxing in the soft spray. Her left index finger circled her clit slowly flicking the ring and putting an increasing pressure on the shaft that held the ring in place. Having stimulation from the bottom and top excited her inflaming her pussy making it pulse, inserting the head of the monster inside she shoved it home its size making her scream her pleasure to the shower walls.  Moving it out and in swiftly brought her off with a massive orgasm that made her drop to her knees shoving the dildo to the hilt butting her cervix brutally. Amiela was beyond caring lost in the pleasure she had found since coming to live with Dillon and Logan, making her a slave for more.  Becoming aware of her surroundings, feeling the water cascading Amiela grabbed the bar on the shower and stood popping the dildo out it fell to the floor.  Shaking from her self imposed orgasm she soaped up rinsing the remains of her pleasure down the drain.  She turned the water off with effort feeling drained, stepping free of the shower Amiela wrapped her body in a large warm towel and walked slowly to the massive bed collapsing on top of the duvet, falling into a deep sleep.

"So how are the preparations coming for the weekend?" Logan asked casually.

"Great, everything is on track, Amiela was exceptionally horny at her milking this morning she came eight times one after the other."

"Hmm and she asked me to fuck her right after she came upstairs. I declined because I was due to meet with you."

"Horny little slut, this is developing better than I had anticipated." Dillon replied with a satisfied smile.

"You think she'll drop her inhibitions and go to any of our guests for relief?"

"Absolutely, I bet she got herself off in the shower."
Logan keyed the computer bringing up the footage for the last
hour of happenings in their shared bathroom, scanning through it
till he came to her entering the shower dildo in hand. Both men
watched through the glass shower wall as she brought herself off
with a lot of moaning and screaming.
"Good, she did as expected, two more days of my special
treatment and she will fuck anyone just in time for the guests to
arrive."
"Perfect everything is moving along, by this time next week she
will be the self assured sexual woman that we both know is there.
It's going to be a pleasure breaking down those walls."
"Now how about we go give her a good fucking?"
Dillon and Logan made their way to the bedroom finding Amiela
face down wrapped loosely in a towel, taking off their clothes she
didn't stir. Pulling the towel away slowly Amiela rolled onto her
back stretching her arms above her head.
Retrieving the handcuffs from the head of the bed he snapped
them on while Dillon restrained her ankles, raising her legs up and
out exposing all her feminine glory to their perusal.
"And what precisely do the two of you think you are doing?"
Amiela asked fully awake and aware with a small smile on her
lips.
"Well we are going to fuck you, as I recall you asked me to help
with your urges this morning." Logan reiterated smiling down at
her taking in how her pussy glistened in the light pouring through
the large windows.
"Oh thank god, I'm so horny I could screw a whole football team!"
"We could arrange a gang bang for you but come to think of it in a
couple of days if you still want it that's exactly what you'll get."
Logan knew he shocked her a little but after all she said she was
horny.
With that said Dillon slid underneath her ramming his huge cock
up her ass with no preliminary while Logan rubbed the head of his
at her pussy entrance teasing her juices to flow freely then
rammed home with one thrust, leaving Amiela gasping and
moaning at the fullness.

Logan began his thrusts while Dillon was stationary, as Logan picked up the pace Dillon began thrusting both were pounding into Amiela giving no quarter. The harder they battered her pussy and ass the more she screamed her pleasure as she plunged into one orgasm so strong she lost all voice. Coming off the strongest cum of her life she dropped into another and another, each more volatile and intense than the last. They exploded together, a unit of pleasure infused flesh and heaving breaths.

In the aftermath they found Amiela had passed out, no response was evident of their efforts to wake her. Logan rose from the bed going off to shower while Dillon poured a glass of water in hopes she would want it when she awoke. Logan returned wet from the shower so Dillon took the opportunity to take his own. It concerned Logan that she was still out but checking her breathing and pulse he determined she was fine and they would wait till she roused on her own.

"I'm going to start dinner, bring her down when she wakes up, wearing as little as possible." Dillon nodded his agreement as Logan took his leave. 'Be a good time to do the last infusion of stimulant while she's out' He thought going into the bathroom retrieving the items he had stored in one of the cabinets earlier. Kneeling on the bed between her bound ankles elevated some two feet off the bed her hairless pussy on full display he took the large hollow dildo inserted the syringe filled with the sexual stimulant and inserted it into her vagina and worked it till it hit her cervix with a few soft pumps he had all the twenty inches inside her, pushing the plunger he emptied the contents inside her body knowing everything inside was well coated with the sexual enhancer. He then took a small wand switched it on and began stimulating her clit while pumping the dildo in and out to achieve the orgasm that would ensure complete absorption. When she began to moan and her pussy clamped down on the dildo he removed everything took it back to the bathroom cleansed his instruments and put everything away.

Upon his return he found Amiela awake enjoying the last of her enforced orgasm.

"Are you alright?" He asked smiling down upon her from the side of the bed.

"Hmm yes." She smiled dreamily back presenting the picture of a well satisfied woman.

"Good, we're going down to dinner shortly so I'm going to get you something to wear then I will release you." He stated going into her closet/dressing room to find her some clothing keeping Logan's orders in mind.  Picking out a completely transparent baby pink baby doll nightgown the would barely cover her ass and pussy with one tiny hook between her breasts to close it Dillon figured it fit the bill.  Hanging it on the opened door he went back undid the cuffs and helped Amiela into the shower.

# Coming Milking

Sitting at the dining table in a short negligee Amiela could only think ' thank god the seats were upholstered, she prayed her libido wouldn't kick in'. It had been more often and she had the strongest orgasms of her life the most recent ones with her men and she had passed out. 'Whatever was going on she loved it and wanted more, it was very addictive to be so sexual and she thought free to be who she now realized is who she was always meant to be.'

Logan set a plate of grilled chicken, tossed salad with his special ranch dressing and glazed carrots in front of her. Accompanied by a large glass of the pinot she loved. As they ate Logan asked.

"Are you ready for this weekend? You are the attraction that everyone is coming to see."

"Yes, I'm ready and I know exactly what I'm going to wear for the kick off on thursday night." She would totally have everyone eating out of her hand.

"Care to share?"

"No, you'll have to wait and find out."

"Something sexy and revealing Amiela no arguments!" Logan commanded.

"You will be pleased, everyone will you'll see." With a secretive smile she continued to eat realizing she would have to be milked soon as the fullness was making matters apparent in the tightness of her night gown.

Dillon cleared his throat ignoring the determined looks passing between Amiela and Logan.

"You will be milked manually by the guests over the next five days, so tonight will be the last time for the machine."

"When are they due to arrive? I have to be milked first thing in the morning or it gets very painful."

"Someone will relieve you in the morning no worries. The guests will be arriving throughout the day, cocktail hour begins at four that's when you will be introduced." Dillon informed her leaving out the fact they were her clients soon to be her fuck partners. She would find out everything over the next few days then they would see where she stood on their way of life.

"I need to be milked now Dillon would you help me?"

"Sure you go on in I'll be there shortly." He waved her away turning to Logan.

"Jake and Matt are in the milking room ready to help with her needs, if I'm correct she will be very accepting of them. If not another dose of stimulant is in order."

"Well let's go see."

They made their way to the door of the milking room looking inside Amiela was standing naked while the two men suckled her breasts very firmly latched on. Both their throats working to swallow all the milk being expelled from her nipples. Both men were hard and standing at attention while their fingers fucked her pussy and ass. Changing position Jake let her nipple go leading her to the sofa by her pussy, Matt followed. He sat on the arm released her pussy then circled her waist with his big hands lifting her onto his generous cock which she slid down seating it inside her, Matt replaced his fingers with his oiled cock making Amiela groan as he worked into place. Jake attached the nipple cups then turned the portable milker on. Milk gushed down the tubes into the collection bottle frothing up as it landed. Amiela's partners then went to work fucking her orifices. Matt slammed into her rectum again and again withdrawing fully to give her stroke after stroke of cock meat. Amiela's orgasm screamed out of her stopping short as another one caught her full force making her shake uncontrollably, her milk being directed to a second bottle as the first was now full. Both men worked their cocks in and out in unison, stamina the order of the night. Logan and Dillon sat in the armchairs watching their lover being fucked to delirious pleasure. She could only feel at this point all her other senses overwhelmed by the electric pounding orgasms she was receiving. Both men gave a few thrusts in quick succession and came with Amiela as she crested her tenth orgasm collapsing into Jake's arms as Matt withdrew. Cum dribbled out of her enlarged anus as he laid her on the cushions withdrawing from her sweet cavern, a flow of her feminine juices followed. Her milk was down to a small stream running down the tubes to the bottle as he turned the milker off, disengaged her milking cups and suckled one breast then the other dry. Wiping his mouth with the back of his hand he gave Dillon and Logan a satisfied look then left the room for his quarters on the upper floor of the house.

Logan picked Amiela up carrying her to their suite to care for her. From the looks of tonight Dillon could hold off for a bit on her treatment, she had no troubling thoughts of proper conduct or prudish ideas when she fucked Jake and Matt who were strangers to her. Obviously her only concern was being attractive to them so they would screw her and give the orgasms she craved. Laying her on the bed he ran the tub then went back scooped her up and placed her in the water loaded with bubbles, a citrus tang found his nostrils which he thought was nice and the stimulant in it would keep her on her search for orgasm after orgasm. Yes their Amiela was a slutty mare wanting to be mounted anytime a male was near. Good he thought as he washed her clean. Leaving her lying back in the tub he retrieved a large syringe filled it with the douche they had specially made. Opening her pussy lips he inserted the syringe till he bumped her cervix, pushing the plunger he emptied it inside washing her clean. He refilled it and did the same to her bowels washing all traces of Matt away. Emptying the tub he took the shower nozzle and rinsed her body while she slept through everything. Wrapped her in a large bath sheet he laid her on the turned down bed and dried her then tucked her in.

Leaving the room with soft moonlight spilling across the bed, he thought she would sleep till morning. He trekked his way down the stairs finding Dillon and their guests in the living room having drinks toasting each other. Jake turned to include Logan in the group as he approached. He took in the hard six foot four body, black hair, a few laugh lines but otherwise the same man all women loved.

"Is she always so superb a lover, so generous?"

"In a word yes and more so on occasion." Logan stated boldly.

"You two are lucky bastards, if you ever need anyone to take care of her for awhile Matt and I would be happy to help."

"I'll keep that in mind Jake.  Let us all enjoy this weekend."

"Hear hear." Dillon replied.

Matt and Dillon met at university becoming fast friends as was the same for Logan and Jake.

"So what's the agenda for tomorrow?" Matt asked Dillon trying to get an idea of how this would all develop.

"Tonight we relax tomorrow morning by nine Amiela will need to be milked, you up to manual or would you rather use the machine?"

"I'm good to sample some more of her, she is delectable."

"Ok then I'll bring her to you in the morning."

"Do I get one on one with her?" Matt asked hoping he would.

"Yes, everyone that comes this weekend will, providing she is acceptable to it."

## Coming Adornments

Amiela awoke alone, a usual occurrence living with two ranchers. It was a beautiful day with sun streaming in the tall wide windows facing east, another identical set faced west giving view to some spectacular sunsets and sunrises over the mountains.

Today they whoever they were arrived, Dillon and Logan had been vague on the guests but she felt up for whatever happened. Her new sex drive brought with it a new sense of adventure. Needing a shower she hopped out of bed making her way to the bathroom turning on the shower, she clipped her hair up while it warmed. Stepping under the spray she thought of last night the sex had been marvelous giving her so many orgasms she lost count before she passed out. Soaping her body, the citrus scent made her tingle all over. Rinsing she turned the water off and was stepping out grabbing a towel when she heard Dillon in the bedroom calling her.

"In here just finishing my shower."

Dillon appeared in the doorway holding a short sleeveless dress with a deep V in the front and one in the back. A broad smile on his face and laughter in his eyes.

"Sapphire blue suits you and the style is very fitting to start your day, I took the liberty of bringing the shoes too." He held up the sparkle blue five inch heels that matched it perfectly.

"Thank you but I was going to wear my robe to breakfast." Amiela replied a little taken aback by his forward attitude.

"I brought that up with me, so you can eat in peace. After you are going to see Matt, he is going to milk you." His statement was casual his body language was ready to break any resistance she offered.

"Oh, I'm not full yet so that is okay. You're escorting me to him?"
"Yes, it's going to be just the two of you this session." Dillon was
excited by the fact he was offering her to another man.
Amiela wrapped the towel around her breasts letting it fall to her
knees, she walked up to Dillon and gave him a soft kiss on the lips
then proceeded by him going to the living area of the suite she sat
in the armchair within easy reach of her breakfast. Pouring herself
coffee she sat back curled her legs under her behind and sipped
the strong black brew. She loved the exotic blend they served,
black was her preference simple, uncomplicated.
"So Dillon how many men are coming to this meet and greet?"
She was determined to get a straight answer before she did
anything else. Dillon looked her in the eye shrugged his shoulders
then sat down taking his time by pouring his own coffee, black.
"At last count we can expect at least twelve, but that doesn't
include any that just show up without confirmation." He broke his
stare with Amiela as he focused on his coffee.
"And am I expected to fuck all of them?" She was a bit shell
shocked by the number, her pussy had other ideas clenching
strongly at the thought.
"That's why they're coming here and to suckle your gorgeous tits.
The first of which is my old friend Matt, he wants you alone so it
will be. It will serve you well to just be and do. You are a natural
slut and once you get going you will love it. You'll get as much
cock as you desire, end of subject. Now its time to get you
dressed as you seem to have no appetite."
Dillon picked up the dress he had laid over the back of the sofa
waiting till she rose and dropped the towel on the floor at her feet.
Looking her over letting his senses feast he saw her glistening
pussy lips and knew she wanted all of it. She had finally dropped
most of her misconceptions about sex and relationships, if she
knew her mother lived a similar life she would be changed forever.
"Go and brush your hair, leave it loose."
Amiela did as told leaving Dillon to ponder the idea of telling her
the truth or perhaps it would be better if her mother came for a
visit and told her. He and Logan had visited Montana many times
in the past few years to sample the mother of the daughter they

now held in their hearts although it had been only recently that he had discovered that fact.  Amiela came back looking fresh with her honey brown hair swirling around her bare shoulders.

"Ok all set." Amiela responded to Dillon's expectant expression. He held the dress while she stepped into it ensuring the fit was revealing enough.  The front V came to her belly button giving glimpses of her ring, having her turn he fastened the hooks at the top of her buttocks leaving most of her back bare.  The length came just below her upper thigh and in front it came just below her pussy lips. The skirt was loose and flowing as the bodice was fitted, the silk material covered her breasts leaving her cleavage and inside swell of her tits exposed, her nipple rings could be seen by the impression they exerted on the fabric.  Here and there all over the dress shiny blue beads twinkled in the sunlight, he placed the shoes at her feet admiring the bead work that matched her dress. Amiela dutifully slipped her feet into the sky high heels testing them out by taking a few steps then turning to face Dillon.

"These are very easy to walk in, I wouldn't of thought so with this band across my toes holding them on but they are."

"You look beautiful and ready to be fucked.  Shall we go."

Amiela swallowed her nerves and meekly replied "Yes."

Taking his arm they traversed the upper floor walking the long corridor from the west side to the east, opening a door Dillon led her into another hallway leading her along, turning down another they entered a large sitting area with doors all around and four additional corridors leading off it, Dillon lead her down another stopping at a large set of double doors, he knocked to announce their presence.  The door slid open revealing Matt with a generous smile.

"Nice to see you again Amiela, come in.  I'LL drop her by your suite when I'm finished.  Thank you Dillon." With that said he closed the door.  Inside the suite Amiela saw a very large bed much like her own in size but this room was very masculine, dark brown woods, hardwood floor to match.  Dark duvet covering the bed with drapes to cover the windows and a tether frame made of intricately carved vines and small animals,  cuffs dangled from the top. Turning to face Matt he answered the question uppermost in her mind.

"Yes, you will be shackled to that frame while I milk those lovely tits and yes you will be naked. Now let me help you out of that scrumptious dress." He unfastened the hooks running his hands up her bare back he took the material off her shoulders letting it pool around her feet.

"Step out now and slip off your shoes."

Amiela did as instructed, standing bare foot waiting.

"Come over here and put your arms out to the side."

When she was in his desired position he cuffed each wrist in turn. She could move her arms up but not down or to the front or back. Matt produced a three foot bar from a storage cupboard and knelt in front of her.

"Spread your legs so your feet sit at either end of this bar."

She did, then he cuffed her ankles to the bar making her wonder if all this was necessary. Reading her mind he looked down upon her from his six foot four height and replied.

"Yes everything I'm about to do is necessary. Your movement is restricted to moving your arms up only. I have a surprise for you as you love big cocks. He went to another door in the wall and disappeared inside, he pushed something out on wheels, placed it in front of her and whipped off the covering. Amiela's eyes went wide at the sight of a huge penis attached to some sort of narrow stand.

"Ok you have taken one this size before, but this one is a little different. For starters its self lubricating to mimic your juices and it expands, once I pop in in you it will go through cycles of larger to larger again than smaller by varied degrees. It also mimics a man's cock by thrusting in and out. Oh yes Amiela we are going to have a great time. Also while I'm sucking one tit the other will be attached to a milking tube, just so we don't waste any of your delicious milk. Your nipples are well developed but your clit needs a bit of extending, so I will attach a lovely little tool to get that done after we're through with your milking."

He moved to her side fingering her nipple rings then moved his hand between her legs toying with her clit ring for a moment earning a gasp from Amiela.

"Responsive slut, let's see how wet you are."

Prodding her outer pussy lips he slid his index finger in to the hilt.

"Dripping wet, you will love the cock."

Withdrawing his finger he put it in his mouth sucking it for a moment then withdrew it wiping it on a handkerchief he took from the pocket of his slacks.

"Very nice, now onward.  I'm placing this cock at your love hole, locking it down so it doesn't move.  Now I'm opening your lips to get the head positioned, ok now I'm going to raise it up with this remote till its three quarters inside your cunt then I'm turning it on. Feeling that baby? Now to fatten it out till it fills your pussy hole, hmmm looks good.  How does that feel?"

"Feels big, I'm.................nggggh......unggh.....stuffed."

"I know wait till I turn it on, but first the collector cup has to be attached to your tit."

Satisfied all was ready he sucked her nipple into his mouth dragging strongly on it for a moment then turned the fuck machine on.

Amiela felt full to bursting as the cock moved in then out.  She felt it expand with a warm spritz of lube, her milk let down and she had her first orgasm, strong and long as the cock pounded away and Matt sucked her tit while toying with her clit ring.  He watched the white milk run down the tube into the collection bottle 'mmm he thought a great fuck slut and a producer too.' Letting her nipple drop from his mouth he attached a collection cup to it and watched her orgasm, making keening throaty sounds of a female getting drilled well and loving it.  He switched the cock to get bigger and then he set it to pounding her pussy. The cock had twenty growth settings that made its girth and length larger, right now he was at four on both.  He could make its girth ten inches and it's length fourteen if he chose.  She was doing fine with the ten inch length so he turned it up to twelve and expanded it to eight inches of girth, that got her attention back on her fuck toy,  he slowed the pounding down to a gentle thrusting to get her used to it and to be sure she absorbed the mare's heat.  It was a special blend that drove women mad to fuck that he imported to season his mares but found it worked just as well on women.  Setting the remote aside on the edge of the frame's support he picked up a jar, opening it he scooped some white cream out with his fingers placing it on Amiela's right breast he massaged it in, then did the same with the other.  He put a dollop on his index finger massaging it into her clit.  Standing back he watched her reaction, she was trying to hump the cock but with her limited movement it wasn't possible.  'Definitely ready to fuck. He thought smiling to himself.  Retrieving the remote he set the thrusting back up to four and expanded it's girth to nine.  After a few moments she was still trying to hump he set the length to maximum, that eased the humping a little, leaving it while he got the collar and clit extender. Coming back he found her hips still gyrating so setting the girth to ten inches he left her while he readied his tools, her moans and screams of pleasure alerted him to her orgasm.  Looking around she was gushing milk into the collectors and the secondary bottle was half full. The cock was thrusting steady and hard at full extension her muscles clenching and she was shaking with the power of it.  Glancing to the readout on the cock base it showed sixteen which meant she had cum that many times. 'Good overall performance, she could easily do a gang bang.'  Observing her reaction to varying the speed he found no change, reducing the girth caused her to hump wildly so he set it back to maximum and watched her relax and sink into another orgasm.

Needing to keep her as still as possible he placed a wide belt around her waist with D rings placed every inch or so. Clipping chains onto six points of the belt he tethered her by clipping the chains to the frame, Amiela was immobilized.  Pulling her clit hood back he exposed it, lovely he thought sweet and swollen with passion.  Picking up the extension tool he placed it over her clit and turned it on,  slowly it moved her clit into the collar after a few minutes the nub popped through the end of the collar holding it securely.  Satisfied he turned off the pump and removed it leaving the collar behind hugging her clit.  He saw Amiela had passed out sagging in her bonds.  Removing her from the frame he laid her on the bed covering her protectively with a quilt.

Picking up the phone he dialed Dillon's cell to find out what the day's agenda was and more importantly what plans they had for Amiela.

"Hey, I was just wondering what Amiela's plans are today?"

"Nothing on until the meet and greet at four.  Why?"

"She passed out after I put her through the regimen you suggested and by the looks of things she'll stay that way for a long time."

"So you collared her clit like I asked and administered the mare's heat?"

"Yes to both and she loved the heat.  I'm not certain she realized I collared her clit, she was really hot.  A small bit before the party will get her burning again no problem."

"Awesome well, take her back to our suite I'll come get her prepared before the party."

"Will do, see you in a few then."

"Ok bye."

Dillon got off the phone happier than he'd been in a long time.  Amiela passed the test, she was a true submissive in the bedroom.  They had strongly suspected this was the case but wanted a Dom to confirm it.

"Is it done?" Logan asked expectantly.

"Yes and she is a true sexual submissive. Matt is coming down to give us a plan for her."

Matt arrived after a while to find Dillon and Logan in the kitchen having coffee which they promptly offered.  With all seated waiting expectantly he began his synopsis.

"As you suspected Amiela is a natural sexual submissive and from this point the best thing to do is encourage her to do everything whether she is completely comfortable with it or not, commanding her if necessary,  just go easy on that at least till she is completely trained.

As I collared her clit with your unique decoration she is yours completely.  The only thing I'm not sure of is if she realized that I did it.  You will have no trouble dealing with that if she doesn't.

Her clit popped through the collar head beautifully and swelled immediately, a nice little cherry sitting on a bed of gold. The swelling has gone down now and she is extremely sensitive as we wished for. She may well have exceptional orgasms just by licking it a little. However we will definitely find all this out over the next five days.

Coming Home Series News

Coming Home Logan's Wish book one

Coming Home Dillon's Destiny book two

Coming Home Amiela's Submission book three

Coming Home Together due out in June of 2014.


Join me on twitter for news updates @aelinemoore or @ARMPublishing

Also on facebook at facebook.com/ARMPublishing


Coming Home Series available on Kobo books, Amazon, Barnes&Noble, Smashwords, Apple, Scribd, Oster, Flipcart, and Google Play and Google Books

# Coming Home Together Book Four
Author: Adeline Moore
Copyright 2014 Adeline Moore

Paperback book published in Canada
Cover art by A.R.M
ISBN:9780991959358

Dedication
Achieving your dream is knowing and feeling you have it.

# Attraction

Amiela woke to the sun streaming into her bedroom through the west windows telling her it was afternoon, glancing at the bedside clock confirmed it was two in the afternoon.  Plenty of time to bath and get dressed before the party, Dillon said it started at four.  Climbing out of bed she noticed an odd tingling sensation in her lower region but pushed it aside in favor of a much needed bath to relieve the tension in her shoulders and back.  The mornings activities were hard on her body taking her back to Matt's bedroom and all the things she had experienced in his hands, making her shiver at the thought of more.  She had decided awhile ago that she loved exploring what made her tick sexually and if all was as Logan and Dillon said it would be she was itching for more.  Turning the faucet on she let the tub fill, getting her lavender bath oil from the cabinet she poured a large amount into the steaming water, breathing the scent relaxed her, calming her over stressed body.  Stepping into the tub she sank down till the water covered everything leaving her head above it.  A moan of complete relaxation sounded in the large room as she shut the water off enjoying the peaceful quiet.

Closing her eyes she focused on the warm water soothing her muscles letting everything unwind.  Drifting in her cocoon of peace and lavender infused warmth she heard her heart beat steady and strong.

Sensing she was no longer alone she opened her eyes to meet Dillon's clear blue ones staring at her.

"Notice anything different?" He had a cocky smile on his face she wanted to kiss off but shrugged her shoulders in answer.  Trailing his hand through the water he unerringly touched her clit making her jump and moan at once. ' That couldn't be right she was never this sensitive.'

"What was that? It was so intense."

"That is the effect of your new clit collar, it keeps you exquisitely sensitive so a little touch can set you off. I'm surprised you hadn't noticed it by now."

Feeling it she found a metal cylinder encircled her clitoris leaving a small cherry sitting on the top. Touching it lightly made her moan.

"When did this get put there and is it removable?"

"Matt put it on you at our request, you passed out from all the orgasms he gave you so I'm not surprised you had no memory of it. And it is removable by us with a special key, but that's not coming off unless there is a need to remove it. So just relax and enjoy how it makes you feel. I'm going to pick your ensemble for this evening, we have a special look in mind for you as you're about to meet the members of the Wild Rose Club."

"What's this club you're referring to?"

"Its a exclusive sex club that Logan and I joined on invitation after graduating university."

"I see, how many members does this club have?" Amiela asked afraid there were hundreds of men downstairs."

"Four thousand plus but we invited two dozen and they all sent their ascent so calm down. These men are the click we hang out with, trusted colleagues."

That said he turned on his boot heel going to select the outfit they had decided she would be wearing. He knew from the look on her face that she wasn't altogether sure about the number of men they had invited but he knew they would treat her like she was theirs. Amiela was a bit shocked but she had to admit excited by the knowledge that she would be the center of attention for this extended weekend. She admitted to herself that she wanted to be a slut for the next several days, let her libido lead her where it may. Stepping out of the tub she dried her skin then put the moisturizer on that Dillon insisted upon. He came out of the closet as she entered the bedroom holding a sapphire blue dress with matching shoes, no bra or panties which didn't surprise her in the least as the dress was suited to going au natural. The dress was halter style with a beaded bodice that would clip at the neck with a gold clasp.  The gold accents followed at the hem embroidered there by an exacting hand into a beautiful swirling design that Amiela recognized from the etching on her nipple and clitoris rings.  She smiled feeling happy and special that they would take such care with a simple dress for her.  Handing the dress to her, Dillon placed the shoes at her feet returning to the closet to select jewelry for her big night.  Slipping the dress over her head and fastening the clasp behind her neck she admired the shimmering blue vision she made in the full length mirror, noticing the hem ended just below the juncture of her thighs.  A lot shorter then she had ever worn before but she liked it turning

this way and that to admire the flattering way it conformed to her body.  Slipping the five inch beaded sandals on her feet she turned extending her long legs to take in the effect of the shoes. Loving the sexy look she turned as Dillon came back with a gem suspended on a short chain.

"This will look lovely on you and show off your cleavage at the same time."

Amiela admired herself in the mirror agreeing with what he had said.  The sapphire did show off her deep plunging cleavage revealed by the halter style dress so much so she thought her breasts might pop out at any moment.

"How about a drink before we join the party?  The guests will all be in the great room in an hour or so, and we are going to make a grand entrance and in that nearly there outfit it will be fantastic."

"A drink sounds wonderful, are you looking forward to watching me get it on with strange men?"  She asked in a teasing tone.

"Yes, we are looking forward to the evening ahead and all that entails." Dillon answered with a secret expression reflected in his eyes.

Watching him pour the white wine into a large wine glass she wondered just what the night would hold.

Taking the glass she drank deeply hoping to calm her nerves, being the only woman in a room full of men was grating and the evening hadn't even begun.

Looking over the rim of her glass at Dillon she asked with raised eyebrows "So what does the evening entail?"

"Impatient I see, you'll find out shortly. But for now come and sit here beside me so we can have a little one on one time before we go down stairs."

"So what kind of one on one time do you want?"

"Just a little wine and conversation. I am not going to mess you up before you have met everyone."

Resting in companionable silence drinking their wine each immersed in their thoughts of the evening ahead.

Meanwhile Logan was seeing to the placement of the final pieces of bondage equipment in the great room, where the party was being held. The guests had been arriving steadily all day being shown to their rooms to settle in before the evening began.

Amiela's grand entrance was set at four providing all the guests were present, glancing at his wristwatch he saw it was three so plenty of time to go and see how Amiela was holding up and get ready for the festivities ahead as Slim and his crew would handle the remainder of the details to be completed.

Taking the stairs two at a time Logan made his way to their suite walking in on Dillon and Amiela kissing passionately on the sofa.

"Hey guys there will be plenty of time for that later! No need to getting her all messed up before the evening even begins."

Dillon and Amiela broke apart with sheepish grins on their faces sipping their wine to cool their ardor.

"Is everything set for tonight Logan?"

"Just about, all the major things are in place, I left Slim and his crew to finish up the minor details while I came and got showered and dressed and to see how you are doing Amiela."

"I'm nervous but considering what I consented to I'm anxious to get on with it."

"Good to hear we'll be taking you down in a little while to meet our guests, won't be too long before you will need to be milked again. We are letting the guests have that honor tonight."

Leaving her in favor of a shower he would let Dillon answer her questions to the how, why and where.

"So Dillon what exactly are you two planning?"

Taking her hands in his, looking into her eyes he stated "You have nothing to worry about, just enjoy."

This reply far from satisfied her but feeling she was getting nothing more out of him she let the subject rest, for all too soon she would find out first hand anyway.

Amiela let her thoughts roam where they may envisioning some threesomes and foursomes in her near future making her hot and very ready if Logan would just hurry up they could go on down and get this evening underway.

If anyone had told her this need to have a three way relationship would take her down this road of supreme sharing a few months ago she would have told them there was no way she would share outside the three of them but here she was about to share herself with two dozen men over the next several days. It showed her just how much lay undiscovered inside her until Logan and Dillon started nurturing her sexual being bringing it into the light of her consciousness.

Logan returned dressed in tan casual slacks and a dark brown button down shirt open to show his throat. No one would ever guess he had deep seated needs to see her being fucked by other men.

Dillon was dressed in jeans, boots and a sapphire blue shirt that almost matched her dress. Button down shirts seemed to be the order of the day she mused, they both had very different choices in colour matching but their style was similar.

"Its time to go down, the party should be well under way by now." Logan stated in his no nonsense way. Dillon held his arm out for her to take and they proceeded through the door following Logan down the hall leading to the staircase.

Reaching the head of the stairs she paused breathing deeply, Dillon gave her a questioning look but said nothing waiting for her to take the next step into her erotic future.

Stepping forward she navigated the stairs one at a time being careful not to stumble in her very high heels. Dillon steadied her with a hand on her elbow keeping to her pace. Taking the last step on the stairs seemed to take forever but was only several minutes in actual time.

Reaching the bottom of the staircase she walked forward with her stomach doing flip flops and her legs feeling like jelly. She had the notion to turn and run back to her suite but it was fleeting and gone as quickly as it had come. Amiela realized she wanted this evening to see if she could do it and if she would love it as Dillon and Logan hoped. She had no doubt this extreme sharing as she referred to it was going to become a very large part of her life.

Logan strode ahead entering the great room bringing everyone to attention with "Gentlemen the reason for this weekend has arrived," Turning he held his arm out indicating Amiela as she came through the doorway on Dillon's arm. Applause erupted all around the room making Amiela wish she were anywhere else but here. She had never gotten used to being the centre of attention hence her choice of profession as a biologist.

Dillon bent down whispering reassurances into her ear, she calmed taking the glass of wine Logan handed to her, sipping lightly enjoying the cold crisp feel dancing across her tongue.

All eyes in the room were riveted on every inch of her taking in the feminine splendor before them.

"Gentlemen Amiela will circulate among you so she can get acquainted with all of you, be patient the evening has just begun." Logan pronounced with a raising of his glass in a toast.

Moving forward with Dillon at her side they joined a group of four men who he introduced as James, Luke, Will and Lucas. Amiela was slightly amazed as two of the men were dark like Logan and the other two fair like Dillon making her wonder if they weren't related in some way.

James started the conversation off with asking about her wolf transplant project slated for completion next spring which animated her persona into the tough biologist she was and not the sex kitten she portrayed physically. Speaking about her work was always easy giving her a great sense of accomplishment.

Dillon was pleased Amiela was relaxing into the evening and excused himself to have a chat with his brother about the events they had planned.

Approaching Logan at the bar he ordered a drink then got down to business.

"So the first order of the night is to have her milked right?"

"Yes, I put James in charge of getting that done, once she has made the rounds then the action as they say will start."

"You're really enjoying this?"

"Yes as are you, I can tell. You know she has been the only one we have gotten this far and with some patience we will be able to go a whole lot further yet."

"I am liking this a lot maybe too much, makes me wonder what I would do if it ended. I don't think I would enjoy that very much."

"Our little girl is into this even though she never in her wildest dreams could have imagined it a few short months ago."

Gazing toward her standing with the last group she was animated and getting slightly uncomfortable as her breasts had grown to swell out of her dress presenting nicely. With a nod of his head James made his way toward her coming to her side, with a touch on her elbow he escorted her to the large arm chair set in the centre of the cavernous room. Once she was seated he stepped behind her and snapped the clasp of her halter style dress open folding the two halves forward to bare her ringed breasts to the assembled guests.

"Gentlemen it is time to suckle from Amiela." He announced as the guests stepped forward to take their turn milking her generous breasts, two of the men started it off by kneeling on either side of her chair and latching onto her nipples. Feeling the suction triggered her milk to let down making her pussy throb with wanting squeezing in on itself unsatisfied. As they sucked her cunt began to cum making her moan and move about the seat of the chair. James held her by pressing downward on her shoulders, Logan came up cuffing her ankles to the legs and her wrists behind her head then tethering her cuffs to a chain he snapped into a ring on the underside steadying her making it almost impossible to move anything except her pelvis. As the two moved away two more took their place until all had their share of her milk. Amiela felt relieved she had been milked but the heat in her sex continued making her desperate for a good hard screw.

James unlocked the cuffs from her wrists and ankles removing them, he scooped her up in his arms and laid her on the bed giving her a few moments to recover while he sorted the restraints laying each in the approximate location it would be used. Removing her shoes he tugged on the hem of her dress pulling it down her legs presenting inches of flesh as it went. To Amiela the removal of her clothing was a relief freeing her sexual animal to the eyes upon her, she was surprised she wasn't embarrassed, but she only felt power in the fact they all wanted a piece of her judging by the bulges she witnessed all around.

Setting her dress and shoes aside James bound her wrists the cuffs fastened to chains that led to the bedposts on either side. The chains extended her arms out giving no slack to bend them, this caused her tits to balloon out and up in perfect position to do with as they wished. He cuffed her ankles in a similar fashion only elevating her legs by clipping the chains on rings halfway up the foot posts of the bed. Now she was on display in perfect position for anal or vaginal penetration and would get plenty of both he thought smiling to himself. Looking around the guests most were now naked ready to fuck with Dillon and Logan's blessing. "Let the games begin" he announced with a sweep of his arm in Amiela's direction.

Two men approached her kneeling on the bed one beside her head the other between her legs, as she couldn't recall their names she referred to them as light and dark. Light rubbed his cock over each of her cheeks then tapped her lips requesting entry she opened her mouth taking him in sucking greedily while dark rammed his long tongue inside her pussy sucking forcefully for a few minutes before he started flicking her clit with his finger, she came hard and long moaning around the cock pumping in and out of her throat. Dark withdrew placing his cock at her pink lips and with one hard thrust buried himself to the hilt, she screamed around the cock in her mouth orgasming again much to dark's approval.

"That's it, you got all twelve inches up you, I bet that feels good. Got a little piece of news for you though it gets bigger as I fuck so you're going to have a really hard ride on this piece of meat but then that will just set things up for the next huge cock you're going to get stuffed with cause you see I'm one of the smaller pricks here."

Amiela gasped around the cock she was sucking off at this but then she came and all thoughts of huge dicks left her mind in the swirling pleasure she was getting.  Light came down her throat and withdrew from her mouth to savour her breast licking and sucking while playing with both her rings which drove her to the heights of another orgasm giving dark the benefit of her vagina contracting brutally on his embedded rod.  He seemed to enjoy it as he came grunting his release then waited while his penis softened enough to withdraw.  They both left her chained to the bed awaiting her next paramours.

The party continued on around her nobody was giving her much notice as she lay chained to the bed her legs spread wide revealing her sex to the assembled guests.  Looking to her left she saw Logan and Dillon talking to a group of six or so, every few seconds they looked gesturing in her direction making her wonder what was next.  James approached her propping her head up to give her a drink of water, waiting while she finished the glass he offered.

"There that's much better I don't want you getting dehydrated. Your next fucking will be starting shortly so just relax and enjoy your free time."  Amiela snorted at that, a very unlady like sound but she didn't care her sex was clenching in on itself making her hornier by the second.  If she didn't get some relief soon she thought she would scream the house down.

Two men stood off to her right, one taking the cuff off her wrist the other her ankle then continued on to the others freeing her.  Jake and Luke she remembered their names from the very animated conversation they had a short while ago.  Picking her up Luke carried her across the room to the binding frame on the far side where he set her down on her feet and cuffed her wrists to each corner while Jake repeated with her ankles spreading her legs wide.

Amiela remembered the last time she had been bound to a frame and all the spine tingling things that had happened made her body lust, wetting the inside of her thigh. She was delirious with sex heat wanting nothing more than to be taken thoroughly by these two men undressing in front of her. Jake stepped behind her positioning the head of his cock at her anus and Luke in front doing the same with her pussy, with a nod of his head Jake entered her in one thrust while Luke followed making her scream from the fullness and pressure she felt inside.

As they moved in and out of her in unison she orgasmed screaming her pleasure to all present in the room, Luke flicked her clit with his finger sending her spiralling into another orgasm on the heels of the first. He kept pumping into her slick pussy and working her clit till she was a moaning boneless woman held only by the chains and Jake's hands holding her waist, careening from one mind shattering orgasm to the next. Her mind spun with all the sensations blocking everything out but the feel of being thoroughly fucked. As another orgasm washed through her system zapping it's way merrily along she passed out, if it wasn't for Jake taking her weight she would have hung there limp and lifeless. As the men withdrew from her body Dillon stepped in behind her wrapping his arms around her body holding her up while Logan released the cuffs.

Picking her up Dillon carried her from the room intent on getting her bathed and into bed, reaching the suite he deposited her in the tub and turned on the water full blast, sponging water over her as the tub filled.

Washing Amiela had always been one of his secret pleasures that he looked forward to every time an occasion presented itself. He took extra care on her breasts and vagina and anus as these had been used thoroughly, satisfied he pulled the plug to let the water drain, picking her up he laid her on the bed. Retrieving a towel from bathroom he gently wiped all traces of moisture from her body. Gently he tucked her in fluffing her pillow, then he noticed she had the necklace on circling the tops of her breasts leading the eye to her cleavage which he found extraordinary every time. They had certainly filled out nicely, like two large melons sitting on her chest, no wonder everyone was anxious to have time with her.

Leaving the room he set the alarm locking the door leaving Amiela in peace to rest undisturbed. It wasn't that they didn't trust their friends with Amiela they did but one never knew who would have a temporary lapse in judgment and end up bothering her in their bed. He walked down the hall comforted in the fact only he and Logan had the code to open the door.

# Abundance

Dillon arrived the next morning as the sun rose, he wanted to get Amiela prepared before everyone started to show up for breakfast, the procedure he was going to perform on her would take an hour to complete at least. Retrieving the exam table from the supply closet he set it by the windows giving her something to look at if she was so inclined.

"Amiela its time to get up?" Shaking her gently she woke taking a moment to focus and orient herself.

"What's up?" She asked sleep still in her voice not quite fully awake.

Picking her off the bed without a word he carried her over and placed her on the table, strapping her hands in place above her head then her feet. Using a remote he spread her legs wide moving the wings of the table her legs were bound to out to the sides giving him plenty of room to work on her pussy and ass. After last night he had decided she was getting the heat to make her a hell of a lot hornier and some stimulant to keep her from passing out. He noticed whenever she became overwhelmed with sexual stimuli she just fainted.

A knock on the door drew his attention away from Amiela as he went to answer it.

"Come in Garrett, I'm glad you could come. Did you bring the devices I requested?"

"Yes, got them right here." He held the bag out for Dillon's inspection.

"Great, she's all set so all we have to do is prime her up a little, I was thinking maybe applying some heat directly inside her vagina, fast absorption maximum effect."

"It will do that and more, I'd be surprised if she didn't fuck the whole guest list before she's satisfied and maybe not even then."

"Let's get started, you set up while I get the heat and the stimulant. She only fucked a few last night I want her to do a lot more today."

Garrett set the bag on the table beside her then revealed its contents one by one. He had a very large dildo he made sure she could see and an anal plug of the same design only smaller. Taking the latex gloves Dillon handed him he snapped them on his hands while Dillon set the jar of heat and a syringe with needle attached beside the items Garrett had set out.

Amiela went to protest but Dillon popped a ball gag in her mouth to keep her quiet.

Garrett handed him a vaginal speculum which he inserted into her vagina, clicking it open gave them a good view of her channel and cervix. Taking a long thin applicator Dillon scooped a large dollop of heat from the jar placing it on her cervix. Garrett handed him another applicator with a generous dollop of heat which he spread around inside her vagina making sure there was a nice liberal coating ready to be absorbed by her body.

Amiela moaned a little as it started to affect her giving them the signs that she was getting the desired amount.

"Now we wait for a bit, its disappearing so it shouldn't be long before we can proceed." Dillon remarked in an offhand manner.

Bucking her hips in a fucking motion earned her thigh straps, and a strap across her waist to keep her still.

"Nice smooth job on her pussy, did you use the remedy the sheik sent over?"

"Yep it works like a charm, she hasn't had any regrowth so far. I think I will do her body again that will ensure none grows."

"He swears by its effectiveness."

Taking a look with a small flashlight up inside her pussy they found only a small trace of the heat here and there.

Dillon took a long cotton swab easing it in until he hit her cervix pumping it back and forth against it her cervix began to open like a flower.

"Give me a swap with some heat on it."

Replacing one swab for the other he placed the heat inside, her cervix bloomed much to Garrett's amazement.

"Awesome that will make it easier for me to fuck her properly."

"I know, and she will enjoy the hell out of it. Not many women do that but this one does and that's all that matters."

Amiela was in a pre orgasmic haze hearing broken phrases and words but not really comprehending them. Her attention had narrowed down to her pussy and the impulses it was emitting.
"Ok time for our little mare to have some fun." Dillon removed the speculum and Garrett promptly eased the head of the massive dildo inside her.
"Hmm it fits ok, tight though but that's all the better for you."
As Garrett eased more inside, her pussy took it, sucking it in. Pumping it in and out had her moaning and squealing around the ball gag but neither of the men paid her sounds any attention. They just observed the transition from empty to a stuffed pussy stretched around the massive dildo. Taking the chains attached to the bottom end of the dildo each stretched one out fastening it to the ring on her thigh strap, ensuring she could not expel it. Next he picked up the anal plug lubed it generously then prodded her anal ring which allowed its entry easing it up her ass. The dildo had a ever increasing width from top to bottom with a groove her anal ring would grab onto thereby holding it in place.
"Nice she took that ass plug well. Its big too so she will have no problem taking a good fucking no matter the size of cock she has to accomodate."
Dillon turned the dildo on letting it pump away gently watching her for signs. When she groaned and squealed around the ball he turned it up to a higher speed.
Garrett turned the anal plug on low then to medium watching her eyes glaze over with passion.
Turning both up to their highest settings they watched her try to fuck the devices back but she was well strapped down and couldn't move, she had to lay their and take as many orgasms as she received.
Dillon swabbed her arm with an alcohol wipe then stuck the needle in emptying it contents into her bloodstream insuring she wouldn't faint.
They left her to the dildos while they went down to the kitchen had coffee and talked.
Logan sauntered in "Amiela getting her heat?"

"Yep well into the process by now its been almost an hour since we applied it." Dillon answered.

"I'll come up with you and watch how she takes the next stage. Some of the guests made certain requests. We'll see if she can do it or not."

Walking into the suite they found her groaning around her ball gag. By the quivering of her muscles she was into a full orgasm, they just watched for several long minutes till she finished. Garrett removed the dildo getting a disapproving groan from Amiela. Putting on a elbow length glove Dillon stepped up to the table shoving three fingers into her pussy to see if the fit was ok. Deciding the anal plug had to go he removed it handing it off to Garrett to clean along with the dildo. Placing three fingers in was easy, withdrawing his hand he placed his fingers together as tightly as possible then worked them into her, it was smooth going till his knuckles touched her pussy lips. Working his hand back and forth and applying some pressure his knuckles eased in a bit at a time, more pressure had his thumb joint inside her then his hand disappeared to the wrist.

"Shall I continue to fist her and get more in, break her in properly or leave that for the guests?" Dillon asked Logan concentrating on fisting her pussy.

"Continue, I want to see how she reacts."

Dillon moved his hand forward getting half his arm in before he hit bottom. His fingers were inside her womb by the way it felt. Amiela was moaning and squealing seeming to be enjoying her first fisting. He felt her pussy contracting as her orgasms continued a steady long stream one after the other.

"Good she took it and she loved it, perfect. Clean her up milk her and put her to bed for awhile. Bring her down for brunch at eleven dressed as we discussed last night."

"Will do, see you later."

Logan left Dillon and Garrett to their chores with Amiela, making his way to one of the guest rooms where he would inform Cedric that yes fisting would be allowed if any of the guests so wished.

Logan remembered he did love to fist his women, this would make him very happy.

Withdrawing his hand Dillon stripped the gloves off threw them in a sealed can under the table meant for medical waste, pulling the milking harness out from under the table he attached her to it and turned it on. She let down and milk gushed down the tubes in a frothy mess, Dillon went to find his clean out kit, he found it several minutes later in the bathroom utility closet. Setting it on the long marble vanity he turned going back to Amiela who was nearly finished with her milking.

Taking it off he popped it into the sanitizing pouch, unstrapping her from the table he carried her into the bathroom setting her limp body into the bath tub. Taking the tube down off the stand Garrett had set up he turned her over.

"Garrett can you hold her up on all fours so we can do the enema?"

He propped her up letting her knees rest on the bottom of the tub while Dillon inserted the nozzle into her anus and turned on the flow. As the bag emptied she moaned at the discomfort of the solution flowing into her. Leaving the nozzle in place it acted as a plug keeping the solution inside to do its work. Pulling the nozzle free Garrett pulled her up allowing her to expel the liquid down the drain. Dillon turned the water on flushing all evidence away, rinsing the nozzle he refilled the bag with clear water as Garrett repositioned her.

Inserting the nozzle into her anus he let the liquid flow, repeating the process until she ran clean.

Filling the tub with water and lavender they watched her soak and relax, washing her clean.

Garrett lifted her limp body from the tub holding her while Dillon dried her then carried her to bed tucking her in, she fell asleep immediately.

Putting all their gear away they left her to rest heading down to the kitchen for a bite to eat and some much needed coffee.

Opening the door Dillon noticed Amiela was still asleep, shaking her gently she awoke, sat up stretching getting her bearings.

"Are you feeling alright baby?"

" Yeah but I'm horny, but otherwise fine. So why do I have to get up again, I really rather would just stay in bed." She used her seductive voice and the look but nothing would sway him.

"Nope we're expected for brunch in half an hour. Don't fret you will have lots of men to choose from to ease your itch."

That perked her up, hopping out of bed when Dillon went into the closet to get her clothing. Coming back he had a baby doll negligee and a pair of heels she could maneuver in.  It was black with fancy intricate lace down the front and around the hem. Helping her into it Dillon stepped in front of her fastening the hook that held it closed between her breasts.

Assessing her reflection in the mirror it was short just falling below the juncture of her thighs with flowing sleeves that ended just above her wrist. The four inch black heels completed the ensemble. There was light and shadow in all the right places making her alluring beyond her wildest dreams.

"You look good enough to eat baby."

"I hope you mean that literally sweet cheeks, I could really use one right now."

"Behave it won't be long, come on lets go down to meet your adoring public."

Leaving the suite they entered the great room a few minutes later to the applause of everyone. Seating her at the head of the table Dillon sat on her right Logan on her left, fielding questions on Amiela's behalf allowing her to answer the one's they chose. She was a bit disappointed, there was no talk of sex. The meal came to an end,  Amiela realized she had hardly touched her food, she wasn't in the mood.

Leaving the table on Logan's arm he directed her to the bed where she lay down, he opened her nightie and left her to hungry looks and leering stares. Her ringed bared breasts and pussy being the focal point.

Garrett came onto the bed taking her shoes off putting them aside, he cuffed her wrists with lots of length so she could maneuver if required.

"Amiela you are here for any of the guests to enjoy for as long as they are interested in having you. And that dildo I used on you earlier is G, he is a bit smaller than me so you are in for a treat when I fuck you."

Nothing happened for the next hour then a small man came introducing himself as Cedric who told her he was going to fist her, looking down at his hands she found they were fairly small like the rest of him. Pulling a glove on he squeezed his fingers together slowly pushing his hand inside then he opened his hand rubbing on her g spot which drove her crazy making her scream so loud and long Dillon brought a ball gag affixing it to her head so everyone could hear each other. Her sounds were muffled but could still be heard pleasing everyone.

Cedric continued pushing into her till he hit bottom and had her squirming, screaming and moaning in a steady rhythm. She came and came with his manipulation of her cervix and g spot until she collapsed onto the bed gasping for breath around the gag. He withdrew his hand complimenting her. "Well done Amiela I can say I have never enjoyed fisting a woman so much, your reactions were divine. I look forward to the next one later today, we will do it a bit differently, but I'm sure I will have you screaming and cuming just as good if not better." He hopped off the bed disposing of the glove in a medical waste canister she had not noticed before.

Dillon was impressed she had stayed conscious with all the stimuli she received, which told him the stimulant was doing its job. if his guess was correct she also was still extremely horny waiting for the next piece of action.

Hans and Adam got on the bed with her one thrust into her pussy hard making her gasp the other just suckled her breasts chewing on her nipples drinking her milk with relish. She was so overcome with sex heat that the particulars of the two didn't matter, her focus was the cock pummeling her giving her one orgasm on top of another until she went limp with sensations so overwhelming she almost fainted.

She came back to herself, she was alone still chained to the bed, everyone seemed to have left the great room in favour of the patio. Hearing voices she looked around, two men approached the bed standing to either side of it. They unclasped her cuffs, one lifted her up with ease and strode to the half barrel shaped device on the far side of the room. Laying her over it face down they cuffed her wrists and ankles to it, her breasts cushioned on the padded surface. Her tummy resting on a bump which raised her ass up giving her captors clear use of her two orifices.

She felt the head of a cock enter her and oh it was a big one, it stretched her even after Cedric had fisted her but no her mind screamed between thrusts it was two cocks working her pussy over together. Her mind spun away on a wave of heat losing all thought, leaving only the sensations of building orgasms exploding one after the other. They blended in her mind leaving her with one unending explosion that continued on and on. She felt others come and use her leaving her limp gasping for air. Some time later she didn't know how long she recognized Cedric's voice.

"Hello Amiela I told you I would be back to give you another fisting, I hope you're ready for this. It is going to feel lovely."

Taking his position behind her she realized he was naked and sporting an impressive cock, if the feeling of it touching her ass was anything to go by. She heard him snap the glove on then the probing fingers entering her pussy slowly easing forward, and his cock at her anus pushing in past the tight ring of muscle. The dual sensations of being filled so full left her breathless and light headed making her scream around her gag as the contractions began sucking both into her body. As before he massaged her g spot then moved his hand forward until she could feel his fingers bumping her cervix which opened allowing his hand into her womb. This time he rotated his arm left to right as he pumped his cock in her ass, thrusting hard. She entered the feeling only realm as her pussy gushed on a cum so big it electrified her body from head to toe giving her jolts as her pussy and ass contracted opening and closing like a fish gasping for water.

With a grunt he came standing still for several minutes then pulled his cock and arm free of her body.

"Excellent Amiela now for the next part."

He probed her ass with his fingers squeezing them together as he pushed forward while pushing something very large into her pussy. The buzzing told her it was a vibrating dildo making her cum hard he pushed into her ass further and further. She was delirious with all the competing sensations making her mind go to the place where her heat roared consuming her in its vortex. Coming down from her sexual high Cedric was gone and someone was unlocking her cuffs, she recognized Dillon's touch but was too tired to care what happened next.

"Let's get you bathed and into bed, you did very well today." Was all he said leaving the room with her in his arms carrying her upstairs depositing her in a tub full of very warm soothing water. Bathing her he told her she had taken anyone who wished to fuck her and loved it as did he and Logan as it fulfilled their voyeuristic needs. Pulling her out of the tub he held onto her around the waist while he dried her skin.

Picking her up he put in the turned down bed covering her then saying goodnight leaving her to rest after her very full day.

Dillon walked into the suite late the next morning to find Amiela sound asleep, getting the syringe from the bathroom cabinet he swapped her arm with an alcohol wipe then stuck the needle in pushing the plunger to empty the contents of the stimulant into her bloodstream.

Grabbing the portable milker from the closet he hooked her up turning it on. Shucking his clothes he climbed into bed pulling her onto his erection wrapping her legs around him, thrusting into her hard let her milk down then her orgasms started expelling the milk from her breasts into the waiting bottles. She roused on a moan but didn't fully wake as her heat took her to the place of flashing lights and tsunami cums, she screamed a bit and moaned but fell back into her deep sleep the moment the milking was done.

# Expectation

Logan opened the door a few inches to find Amiela sitting up in bed her breasts bare the blanket huddled around her waist. She looked wide awake so he assumed she had been up for awhile.
"Hey baby are you feeling better?"
"Yes I do, I just conked out, I don't even remember lying down."
"Well that's alright you took to the heat remarkably well but it took more out of you then he realized so this afternoon you'll be spending with Garrett instead. Are you ready for that?"
"He is a man Logan and I do need a man desperately!"
Amiela sounded agitated with sexual frustration which was good, Garrett was no easy pick for a woman to have sex with but she did well throughout all the preparation so he had no doubt she would glow in this as well.
"Time to get ready, you go and shower but leave your hair dry."
As she headed to do his bidding he went and found a dress shoes and jewellery for her to wear on her date.
Amiela was waiting for him when he stepped into the bedroom.
"That was quick, I found everything you're going to need. I'm guessing you are anxious to get this underway."
"Well yes, I'm horny as hell and need sex. Your fault by the way you wanted me this way so just give me the dress and let's get on with it."
Logan handed it over with a gigantic smile on his lips.
Amiela looked it over with a critical eye red not exactly her colour with a shimmering effect, looking closer she saw silver and gold threads had been woven into the silk. Not much to it, a band would go over and around her chest and braided threads led off it down to the tiny skirt. Turning it she found the only solid piece of material down the back where the zipper was attached and the skirt might cover her butt but not much else. Looking over at Logan with a you have to be kidding me right, he just shook his head in a negative response holding up the six inch stiletto heels with a red, silver and gold band where her toes would slide through to hold them on her feet. Removing the dress from it's

hanger she unzipped it, stepped into the tiny confection sliding it up and over her breasts, placing her shoes on the floor Logan stepped behind her zipping it up.

"Well it feels more comfortable than it looks and surprisingly my tits don't pop out."

"It's eye candy for Garrett, he likes things like this. Now on with the shoes, and these."

Turning she found him holding four bracelets made of gold with platinum etchings to match her nipple rings and clit collar, about an inch and a half in width and sturdy, with a ring on each that moved up and down.

"These are yours Garrett brought them, so on with the shoes and then i'll put these on."

"Something else I can't remove on my own I suppose?"

"Yep slave bracelets can only be applied and removed by the master."

Amiela thought he was kidding about the slave term but the bracelets would do the job of securing her if a chain were clipped onto them. Standing in her new glittery shoes she watched as he clipped one of the bracelets to her left wrist and then her right, they felt cold against her skin giving her a thrill at their application. The heat started to rise as he put one on her left ankle and continued to consume her as the right ankle was placed in the bracelet.

"Turn around and look at yourself in the mirror."

His commanding tone had her cumming bending her knees to keep from falling and riding the orgasm through. Gripping her in it's pulsing, grinding sensations she panted and moaned then screamed as it peaked and a second started taking her along to a height she had never felt with a strength that knocked the wind out of her body and every thought from her mind. Feeling was all she could do.

"Good orgasms Amiela you're progressing nicely."

Looking at her reflection she looked every inch the collared and cuffed slave right down to the tiny skirt playing peekaboo with her pussy.

"Excellent slave your new jewellery suits you and it will be much easier to secure you to anything at any time."

Standing behind her he took her wrists in his big hands clipping the rings on her bracelets together effectively restraining her hands behind her back.

"Now you're ready lets go see Garrett for a session you will never forget."

Gripping her upper arm he led her out of the suite down the long wide hall turning left into another

hallway with doors opening off it on either side then right for a short way till they came to a large set of doors which Logan knocked on twice in quick succession.

Garrett opened the door standing there smiling down on her his massive body dwarfing hers.

"Hello Amiela, Logan come in."  Standing aside to let them pass.

"Here she is as you requested slave cuffs and all." Logan smiled shaking the hand Garrett offered.

"Very nice, it will be most helpful.  Now if you will excuse us we have a lot to do."

"On my way see you at dinner, the great room six o'clock."

"See you then."

Garrett closed the door after Logan turning to Amiela he looked her up and down and around an approving nod here a smile there. She was about to scream at him to say something when he spoke.

"Do you remember what I told you?"

"Yes, that G was big but not as large as you."

"Very good, you must be ready for me then."

Garrett was wearing a pair of loose jogging pants but even they couldn't hide an impressive package straining to get free.  Untying the drawstring he slipped them down his legs kicking them aside, standing waiting for her to take in all the details.

Amiela gasped at the size of the penis in front of her it had to be twelve inches and it was as thick as a pop can with a huge head reminding her of a portobello mushroom and it was soft.  What would it be like when it was hard.  Oh my god, oh my god, she chanted silently in near panic which changed to lust and heat in a moment of clarity, she wanted that monster in her.

Garrett watched the changing emotions on her face and knew the second she found carnal interest.

Stepping around behind her he unclipped the cuffs with a flick then massaged her shoulders and back to work the stiffness out. He knew that even after a short time the arms and back tended to stiffen when one was not used to it, she would get there but it took time and practice.

Being in close touching her stirred his cock to semi hardness brushing her buttocks so he slid it between her thighs and worked it a bit to find out how hot she was. Removing it and stepping back there was moisture coating it where he had touched her pussy.

Moving around he stood in front of her noticing her eyes were on his cock, Logan and Dillon had done a good job with her so far now it was up to him to show her some new things.

"No time like the present to get started on a new phase for you Amiela." His voice brought her eyes to his face questions written there.

"Look around there are a few things in here you have not seen before I'm sure. Tell me."

"Well there is the chest and the kneeling bench. Nothing else seems out of the ordinary."

"True but sight can be deceiving such as the chest, come let me show you."

Crossing the room to the chest he took her arm directing her closer "Lay down on your back hands at your sides."

Once she did he pulled a narrow panel out vertical to her shoulder, taking her wrist he positioned her arm on top clipping her cuff into a ring set in the wood. He secured her other arm then stood between her knees knelt down and pulled a telescopic pole out of the bottom of the chest then another. Taking her ankle he secured the cuff to the pole so her knee was bent and fastened the other in the same fashion.

"Now I have you secured I can move either of these poles in or out which means I can spread your pussy open to my liking or not. I can present your ass in any way I like as well."

Pushing a button on the top corner she felt her hips lifted by several inches presenting both of her orifices to be used in any way.

"And the final adjustment, I can raise or lower the bench to accommodate the height of the man using the slut on the bench." Flicking a switch on the chest it rose stopping when his cock head lined up perfectly with her slit.

Amiela was mortified to be called a slut by him but then she realized it was only a reference and he hadn't called her the slut so she was ok with that. In her mind it was one thing to be called slut by Dillon and Logan they cared for her and therein lie all the difference.

Garrett produced a blindfold from the chest moved to her head and put it in place blocking out all light and fastened it behind her head.

"You can only feel and smell, this will take you closer to your sexual centre thereby causing you stronger longer orgasms."

Garrett squeezed his fingers together into a cone shape moving them up and down her slit making her moan, sliding the tip of his middle finger inside had her bucking he withdrew. Leaning over the chest he found the restraint pulled it out adjusted it and snapped the ends together across her waist.

Resuming his position he slid the tip of his middle finger into her wet pussy again, this time she tried to buck but her restraint held firm. Pushing his hand forward a little he found her tight but pliable, working his fingers back and forth he gained a bit more of his hand inside her. All four fingers were inside as he worked his hand pushing forward easing back pushing forward until his thumb slid in and out easily. Pushing his hand in his knuckles disappeared then his hand slid forward to the wrist.

Through all the probing Amiela was in ecstasy her pussy throbbed and squeezed cumming again and again producing cries of pleasure and completeness.

Garrett was very pleased as he withdrew his hand, watching as her pussy contracted, her face a picture of sublime ecstasy.

Taking his cock in hand he rubbed the head up and down her slit several times, touching her clit with his fingertip massaging it gently getting moans of pleasure.

Plunging half his cock into her in one motion rewarded him with a scream and more gusty moans. As she began to pant he pushed into her then out then in setting a steady rhythm gaining more depth as he pumped. Bumping her cervix he continued to bombard her with his monster cock then it flowered open enough he could feel it. Continuing the stimulation she continued to dilate till the large mushroom head slipped into and past her cervix her womb accepting him home.

Her screams of pleasure and vocalization drove him higher than he had ever been, more blood pumped to his cock making it bigger and she was accepting him all of him. As he worked his cock into her and out setting a steady rhythm she was taking a full stroke every time and by the sounds coming from her and the clenching of her cervix and vaginal walls she was hot for him and getting hotter.

Clenching his butt muscles to keep from cumming thinking if other things was mute he roared and came harder than he ever had with Amiela screaming her orgasm long and hard.

At the end of his catastrophic experience he was panting and moaning along with her as his cum pumped into her spurred on by her clenching and squeezing of his big rod.

Softening his cock began to shrink out of her, he removed himself leaving her going into the bathroom to rid himself of the condom he always used for his sexual encounters.

Coming back to her he saw she was clenching her fingers.

"That was the best fuck I've ever had baby, you are fantastic. I can see why Logan and Dillon love you so much, I would too if you weren't already taken."

Walking to her feet he watched her pussy still working its way through the monster orgasm he had bestowed upon her.

Leaving her he set up the horse she was going to be using next. Coming back he noticed she had calmed and her breathing had steadied, taking off the blindfold she blinked her eyes several times in the low light and focused on his face.

"Hey there baby are you alright?"

"Yes I'm good." She replied her voice a bit hoarse from the screaming she had been doing through her orgasms.

"I'm going to release you and help you out of your dress, we are not done yet. I hope you're up for that."

"God I hope not I'm just getting started, I need more, the heat is just too big."

"I've got more for you little lady no worries." Garrett replied chuckling at another first, no woman ever wanted more than one session with him. He would have to apply the techniques Dillon was using when he acquired his own woman.

Releasing her ankle he set her foot on the floor then busied himself with the other and up to her wrists. Freed she didn't move until he coaxed her to sit by taking her hand and giving it a gentle tug. She stood with help but her legs were shaking, releasing the zipper on her dress it pooled around her feet, stepping out of it he picked it up and laid it on the chest still warm from her body. He noticed her shoes laying where they fell from her feet, sparkling merrily in the low light.

Nudging her forward with a hand to her back he directed her to the base of the horse he would bind her to.

He guided her onto the horse, straddling the narrow top piece her body would rest on leaving her breasts to swing free on either side. She placed her knees on the supports provided and her hands were pressed palm down on the top supports. She was basically on her hands and knees with a frame to bind her to.

Clipping her wrist cuffs to the snaps provided he proceeded to clip her ankle cuffs in place then he strapped her legs to the frame just below the knee, and ran the strap across her waist to keep her from bucking too violently. She had a finite range of movement all to enhance his sexual experience and dominance over her.

His cock reared to full mast from the sight of her beautiful ass presented so invitingly.

Stepping in he ran his cock on her anus then pushed half the enormous head inside her hearing her gasp he sunk more in making her push back and emit a keening wail. Going all the way to the hilt had her pussy dripping cum all over the floor as she convulsed moving her ass in sync with his thrusts.

Feeling his balls tighten he let the orgsasm take him spurting his seed in a long torrent having him gasping for air. Giving his cock one last thrust into the tight passage he withdrew spent for the moment leaving Amiela in the throes of the biggest orgasm thus far.

Looking over his shoulder he was struck by how beautiful she was in the grips of pleasure.

Coming back she was still, her breathing still ragged but steady. Wiping her clean he threw the cloth on the floor wiping it clean with his foot, then patted her ass dipping all his fingers into her pussy getting a ahhhhhhhhhhhhhhhhhhhhhhhhhhhhhhhhh god that feels good. Pushing in he buried his fist in her pussy working her a bit more his wrist disappeared and a third of his forearm. Satisfied he worked his arm back and forth in and out until she exploded in a frenzied clenching cum squeezing out onto the floor coating his hand and arm.

She slowed and then stopped her squeezing then he withdrew going to the bathroom to shower after his exertions leaving her tethered to the horse awaiting what came next. As he showered he thought back over all the acts he and Amiela had performed knowing that Logan and Dillon would be pleased with her progress, the hard orgasms she had one after another only for the next to be harder and longer still, they had spent hours fucking just the way he preferred because once was never enough for him.

Rinsing himself off he stepped out drying his body with a large fluffy heated towel from the rack, tossing it in the hamper when he finished. Brushing his short hair and brushing his teeth he wondered how she was doing? She hadn't passed out once which was good, Dillon must have given her the stimulant to prevent that.

Entering the bedroom/playroom he found her asleep, exhausted was more likely. Removing the straps and unclipping her cuffs he lifted her from the horse carrying her into the bathroom where he deposited her limp body in the tub full of warm water he had ran.

Washing a woman was a particular favorite of his and this one had more than earned the pampering. She hadn't roused by the time he was finished so he picked her up set her on the vanity and dried the moisture from every inch of her skin. Discarding the towel he picked her up and carried her to the bed where he covered her up with a quilt and left in search of Dillon and Logan taking care to set the automatic lock only he could open with his fingerprint.

Walking down the hall he met Logan going into his suite.

"Hey you may as well come in we'll have privacy here to talk, I take it that's why you're here?"

"Yep thought we could go over a few things concerning Amiela."

"Great Dillon's inside."

Entering they found Dillon coming out of the dressing room holding a purple dress with shoes to match.

"Hey Garrett you enjoyed yourself?"

"Hell yes she was amazing, I've never known a woman like her."

"We feel the same way, now what do you want to discuss?"

Garrett took a few moments to gather his thoughts "Amiela took everything I had and demanded more besides which I gave her, she was submissive to a fault, perfect in fact.

The heat gave her a freedom I have never seen in another or taken the condition so well.

All she wanted to do from the moment she saw my cock was to have it."

"We thought she would, we can do anything we want sexually speaking to her and she revels in it. Do you think we should commence with making her a full fledged slave or just leave her as she is?"

"Man don't fuck with perfection, she wears the collar and the cuffs and loves them but no making her a slave would be a mistake you both would regret. There are plenty of other women you can do that with. What I want is to keep her with me this evening if that's possible?"

"I don't see any problem with that we can milk her in your suite tonight away from the other guests and one phone call to the club will send several women for the others to use.
So yes she can."
"It's fine by me as well Garrett but what are you planning to do to her?"
"Fuck her senseless what else, she fell asleep but in an hour or so she'll be awake and wanting more, the heat has that effect on her. One more thing let's get James to come and change her clit collar, I found a terrific little collar in Amsterdam and knowing you guys would probably put one on Amiela I bought it for her. She will be more sensitive than she is now and will love it. Can we get that done tonight? "
"I will tell him to come to your suite by five and get it done both Logan and I will be there shortly before."
"Great I will see you shortly." Garrett left the suite making his way back to Amiela.

Opening the door he found her asleep in the same position, going to the bed he brushed the hair off her face touching her reverently never had he found a woman who so enamoured him as this one did. Sex aside there was something about her that he couldn't get enough of. Sitting beside her on the bed he watched her she was having a dream, her face went from euphoric to serene, it was a happy memory, maybe she was dreaming of him.
Looking down he noticed it was four forty five Dillon and Logan would be here soon.
"Amiela baby its time to get up. Come on now let's go." He stroked her face to aid him in waking her. She opened her eyes blinked rapidly several times then just looked at him with the sweetest smile on her face.
"What's up? I want to sleep some more, you really wore me out."
"I know later I promise but Dillon,Logan and James will be here soon, so get up please." How could she refuse when he was being so nice to her.

"Alright, I'm getting up." Sitting up bared her breasts to his view which he was very appreciative of giving them a thorough going over with his eyes then he remembered the box.

"I bought something for you, here open it."

He held a small ring box that made her heart flutter. Opening the hinged box she found a small ring inside, it was too small for her finger however so she knew it was for her clit.

"I have one of these, so what's this one for?"

"It will be more comfortable and will have some pleasurable effects that you will love. Trust me ok."

"Ok, so James is coming to swap them?"

"Yes and this time you will be awake for the procedure."

That caused a ripple of fear to radiate through her but she did trust what Garrett had said so she would take whatever pain or discomfort came. Looking at the ring nestled in its red silk bed she wondered if what he said was true, she hoped so. It was thinner like a babys ring, gold with an etched design in silver or maybe platinum. It also had the M lock and the key lay beside it.

"So you like it I trust?"

"Yes its beautiful thank you."

"You're welcome." He rose went into the bathroom and came out with a silky plum coloured robe made of silk.

"Come here I will help you put this on." He held it out so she could slip her arms through the long sleeves. Took her hand and seating her on the couch in front of the fireplace, he was about to say something but just then a knock sounded on the door so he went and answered it instead.

"Come in." Logan, Dillon and James came inside exchanged pleasantries then James went back outside and wheeled in a chair much like you would see in a dentists office only this one had legs supports and straps much like a gynecologist's table.

"Come here Amiela and sit in the chair." Garrett directed so she did.

James cleared her robe back to reveal her legs and torso then strapped her leg in at mid thigh and ankle then a strap went around her waist and clicked closed and finally her wrists were secured to the chair arms. Pumping a lever on the bottom of the chair laid her back at a lounging angle and raised her hips, widening the legs supports he spread her wide open so everyone assembled could see her charms.

James took the key unlocking her clit collar removing it, then he reached under the chair producing the suction system Dillon had used to lengthen her clit and nipples. She noticed he was wearing surgical gloves wondering why? Garrett produced the new ring which James took and popped it into the end of the suction tube, there was a groove which held it in place. Placing it over her clit Dillon switched it on and within a few seconds her clit had been stretched through the ring into the cylinder the suction pulling her clit out stretching it a bit more. With a nod from James, Dillon switched it off, James then removed the tube putting it back under the chair.

"All Done Amiela that wasn't too bad now was it?"

"Only a slight discomfort, but this ring makes my clit feel hot and tingly."

"As it should." Garrett replied "It's infused with a stimulant that will enlarge your clit about one size larger than it is now. You will adore it a bit later trust me."

She nodded but said nothing more wondering when she was getting milked, her breasts were getting uncomfortable.

"Now I think its time you were milked, Dillon did you bring the milker?" Garrett asked.

"No need there's one here in the closet." Leaving for a moment he came back with a portable version of the one she used in the milking room. A bottle on each side with the suction machine in the middle with the milking tubes and breast cups coiled up on a clip waiting to be stretched out and used.

"Here you go, you may as well do the honours, I bought these new milking cups and I want to observe how they work." Dillon handed the machine off to Garrett who set it on the floor. Opening the top of her robe revealed her very large breasts, palming one it felt very warm but normal he decided going to the machine he uncoiled the cups and tube applying the milkers to her breasts Logan turned it on.

"They will stay put with the suction, see her nipples fit down into the tube there perfectly." Dillon remarked to Garrett who took his hand away.

After a few seconds the milk started to dribble down the tubes, Dillon stepped forward shoving all his fingers into her pussy, with a long moan the milk started to flow faster. Working his hand in further up to his knuckles set up an even flow, when her pussy swallowed his wrist and started squeezing the milk gushed faster.

"You see the closer she gets to cumming the faster she expresses her milk, the two are forever linked and will always work in unison."

Dillon began a slow fucking motion with his hand causing Amiela to pant and wail until she came screaming out her pleasure and the milk poured like a river down the tubes into the waiting bottles. Handing Dillon a dildo with a clit tickler Logan commanded he put it in her so they could all sit back have a drink and watch as she lost her mind in orgasmic bliss.

"She really likes being milked it seems." James stated smiling a wolfish smile that the other men knew very well.

"She didn't at first, it took a while for her to come round to it but since then she had revelled in it every time." Logan remarked smiling enjoying Amiela's reactions and sounds and having the others watching her too.

Dillon handed drinks all round and sat watching and listening to his lovely little mare being milked.

"Where did you meet her?" Garrett inquired innocently thinking if there was another even remotely like her she would be the one for him.

"Her mother and fathers sent her here, we know them through the club. Anyway she studies wolves for transplant and her mother thought it would be a good idea for her to come up here and study ours with a transplant in the offing. There was a two fold agenda though the second being Logan and I. We meet get to know each other and if all went well then we initiate her in the ways and customs of the Wild Rose Club. And the rest is history, we each knew the moment we met her that she was ours and her agreeing was a bonus."

"So she is the product of a tri relationship, any siblings?"

"Two brothers, married with children of their own to a lovely young woman. Amiela is actually the product of a foursome but the third father passed away when she was just a baby."

Garrett sat sipping his drink digesting what Dillon had told him and wondering if there was room for him in their lives when he was home, or better yet have Amiela travel with him sometimes.

"What is the stimulant the ring was coated with and will it interfere with her other regime?"

"Naturally occurring in the female body so no it will be fine, all it does is stimulate her clit so it will mushroom around the ring, her clit will get bigger and the ring is much more comfortable than the collar. You can apply the stimulant anytime you notice her clit shrinking but once a month is all that is required to maintain it's size. I brought a bottle with me so you will be well supplied and by tomorrow her clit will be a lovely plump little mushroom cap."

"What about her sensitivity?"

"Off the charts."

"Perfect we have a lot to look forward to. The women from the club arrived and are entertaining downstairs so no one will bother you for the night, dinner will be brought up shortly with Amiela's favourite wine. If there's nothing else, I think we should be going. You can disconnect her when she's finished?"

"Absolutely, and Dillon thank you for honouring my request."

"You're welcome no problem." Dillon replied with a gleam in his eye.

After the men left Garrett returned to Amiela kissing her forehead, she was almost done. He would send the milk with whoever brought dinner he thought. And after they had eaten he would spend some very good quality time with her, his smile broadened and his mood became very light just thinking about it.

After he had taken her off the milker and was getting her settled on the couch a knock sounded. Logan smiled at him as he opened the door.

"Dinner is served." He wheeled in a cart with their dinner, several silver topped dishes decorated the surface with a bottle of pinot chilling in a silver ice bucket and a bottle of red.

"Wow thanks this is great." Garrett stated enthusiastically.

"You're both welcome, I'll just grab the milk and go."

He grabbed the machine and headed out the door before anything more could be said.

"He was in a hurry, that's not like him, he will usually exchange greetings and a bit of small talk before he rushes off." Amiela remarked drily from her spot on the sofa.

"Would you like some wine or have dinner now with the wine?"

"Wine now please."

Garrett filled a glass of white and one of red carrying them to the sofa, he handed the white to her.

"So what am I doing here, I thought I was to show for dinner with the guests and be milked?"

"Change of plans I requested you spent the night with me and Logan and Dillon approved
readily I'd say."

"And what about the guests, what are they going to do?"

"They are being entertained no worries Dillon took care of it."

"Ok that's fine, I like you and we did have fun together."

"Are you ready for round two with me?"

"Not yet I'm sated for the time being, milking always does that to me. At first it knocked me out and I'd sleep for hours after, but the longer I do it the better it gets. What is it you do Garrett?"

"I'm an engineer, I work abroad for the most part about four months a year, when I'm home I run a ranch horses mostly, some cattle still. My spread is about forty miles from here as the crow flies, sixty if you take the roads."

"So you know Logan and Dillon well I suppose?"

"We grew up together went to the same schools, our parents were very good friends."

"So where are your parents now?"

"Passed away, five years ago now in an auto accident."

"I'm sorry I didn't mean to bring up sad memories."

Taking her hand in his he kissed her knuckles giving her a reassuring smile.

"It's ok I'm past it now all I have are cherished memories when I think of them."

"That's good, one of my father's passed away when I was five, I still remember him but like you they are good memories."

"How many father's do you have?" He asked earnestly not to give away that he already knew.

"Two my mother married three brothers. Does that shock you?"

"Not at all I've always been a live and let live kind of guy. The decisions people make for themselves are what's best I think. Your mother is a good example she found what she wanted and took it, more people should be like her."

"My mother is a rare find and my father's are still head over heels in love with her."

"As are you a one of a kind find." Amiela blushed at the compliment, she still wasn't taking them very well.

"Thank you, I would love to eat now if you're ready?"

"I can always eat, anytime."

Setting their glasses aside they went to the cart and removed the covers to find shrimp salad, strawberries and whipped cream, an assortment of cheese, fruit and crackers.

Garrett took half the plates Amiela the other and set them on the coffee table in front of the couch. He went back for the wine and refilled their glasses.

Garrett found many reasons to touch her it seemed from feeding to kissing to having his hand resting on her thigh, he was possessive she could see that but why she wasn't with him other than in a sexual way ok friends too she admitted to herself.

"Would you like more to eat Amiela?"

"No, I will just finish my wine."

Garrett watched her admiring her in many small ways and when she finished her glass he announced.

"Come with me." He held his hand out helping her up, they walked to the side of the bed where he took the robe off her shoulders baring her to his view.

Stripping the duvet, blanket and top sheet to the bottom of the four poster bed he motioned for her to get on it. Crawling on the bed with her he retrieved the chains from the head of the bed and secured her cuffs to them.

"I'm not securing your feet just yet, I want you mobile."

She found she could move her arms about halfway down her body but she couldn't bring her hands together to remove her cuffs from the chains.

Garrett undressed and joined her she noticed he was erect his monster cock bumping against his tummy. Rolling on a condom he positioned himself between her legs wrapping them around his waist. Lining the head up with her slit he slowly entered her just a little at a time giving her a moment to adjust to him. Working his cock in he finally managed to feed all of it to her, he was well embedded inside her body and at the moment wanted nothing more. Too soon his body demanded he move. He began pumping her slowly taking her nipple between his lips he sucked strongly. Amiela was in heaven her orgasm blooming going off in a myriad of colours behind her eyelids. Garrett felt it, pumping into her hard in a bid to reach his own. She headed straight into another one as he massaged her clit, and another as he slammed back inside going through her dilated cervix into her womb. His balls tightened and then off he went pouring his semen into her waiting pussy. Garrett wanted nothing in that moment but to stay just as he was. Propping himself on his elbows to keep his weight off her he kissed her long and lovingly taking in every nuance of the wine and her taste.

Rolling to the side he snugged her into him laying with her listening to her breath savouring the feel of her soft feminine body touching his hard masculine frame.

"Why don't we just snuggle for awhile maybe go for round three a bit later?"

"Sounds good I need a rest." She sounded sleepy and he would let her rest snuggled next to him.

Releasing her from the chains and tucking them away he pulled the folded blankets up and over them, she immediately turned to her side pressing her back into his front, he brushed her hair to the side with his hand giving him direct access to her throat. Kissing her several times had her moaning lightly he stopped, tucking her breast into his large hand snuggling down he fell asleep as she did.

## Celebration

Amiela awoke as the first rays of light hit the horizon glowing just outside the window. Turning over within Garrett's arms she kissed him gently, knowing he was awake when his tongue invaded her mouth deepening the kiss to an intimate coupling.

"Good morning beautiful, did you sleep alright?"

"Deeply, I feel completely energized and I'm hungry again."

"For food or me?" He teased not sure which she was referring.

"Breakfast, no one should be up yet, do you want to go and raid the refrigerator and help me make something?"

"Sounds like fun, let's go."

Amiela donned her robe while Garrett pulled on his jeans and a t-shirt from the dresser.

They tip toed past the occupied rooms , past her suite letting out a breath of relief when they reached the head of the stairs. Walking down hand in hand they crossed the living room keeping an eye out for anyone.  Entering the kitchen all was clear, Amiela headed for the refrigerator pulling out ham, cheese, peppers, onions while Garrett found a few spices in the cabinet beside the stove to add to the omelets.

"Bacon and toast too?" Amiela inquired of Garrett.

"Why not we worked for it."

Amiela blushed remembering what they had done together, one look at the table had her reminiscing about what she and Dillon had done on it.  Get a grip she told herself its sex nothing more.

Garrett didn't comment on her blush just busied himself chopping the veggies and grating the cheese.

"Would you beat the eggs? I have the bacon going, you can make the toast." His voice was light teasing, and for such a dominant man it was nice to see he had a boyish side and could show it to her. A light feeling sprang inside her making her wish she could keep this Garrett forever.

Beating the eggs thoroughly she handed the bowl over so he could add the other ingredients to make the omelettes, pulling the toaster out of the cupboard she found the all natural multigrain bread they loved and popped it in the toaster.

"Multigrain ok with you?"

"Ya that's fine." Garrett replied smiling then returned his attention to the omelettes putting cheese on and folding them over.

Amiela set the table, laid out some fruit and yogurt then turned back to the toast buttering it and pouring coffee and orange juice. Garrett put the bacon, toast and omelettes on a platter and brought them to the table seating himself beside Amiela. Holding the platter for her she took the food she wanted then added some cantaloupe, strawberries and yogurt to her laden plate.

"You can eat all that?" Garrett asked motioning toward her plate.

"Yes, lactating starves me, it takes a lot of energy to produce milk, and I'm still losing weight no matter how much I eat."

Garrett was concerned about the weight, perhaps a little less milk production was in order so she could maintain her weight because in his opinion she was thin enough. She probably wouldn't get pregnant unless she gained a little. Shaking his head he wondered where in hell that thought came from, he had never even considered being a father much less impregnating Amiela. She dipped a piece of cantaloupe into the yogurt offering it to him bringing his thoughts back to her as he closed his lips over the fruit nipping her finger for good measure. Snatching her finger away she stuck it in her mouth soothing it with her tongue, the action had his libido roaring to the forefront making him instantly hard. He gave her a strawberry holding it while she took the two bites necessary to finish it. It was a pleasure being with her even over breakfast and if wishes came true she was his one wish for always. Lost in their intimate world of good food, great conversation and reading every nuance of each other they were startled when a voice came from behind them.

"You two seem to be getting on great, care to share?" Dillon remarked walking by on his way to the coffee maker.

"Good morning and no I don't, just breakfast between good friends." Amiela rebutted him waiting to see if he would comment on her being with Garrett further. He and Logan had orchestrated it anyway and be damned if she was going to feel guilty for having fun. On second thought why did she feel as though she were cheating on him and Logan? Because stupid your heart is involved with Garrett. Did she love him? That was the million dollar question all she knew was she didn't want this morning to end.

Noticing her lost in her thoughts Dillon chose to say nothing further as he came and sat down across from them at the table.

"Garrett are you still planning on staying for the week ?" He asked raising his eyebrows in question.

"Yep, we still have some stock to look at before I make any final decisions on which of the mares and stallions I will buy."

"Well good we can go take a look tomorrow, all the guests will be leaving in the morning except James he's staying on for a couple of extra days."

"So what are the plans for tonight?" Amiela asked knowing her heart wasn't in for anything more than dinner and some conversation.

"Just a farewell dinner and a bit of a party, I think most of them are worn out after last night." Dillon replied smiling at the memories of the club women giving them a thorough going over.

"Partied a little hard?" She quizzed him wanting to know what they all did last night.

"You could say that, look I'm going to tell you something just wait till I'm finished to comment ok?"

"Alright what is it?"

"After Garrett requested your presence last night I called the club and had them send out some women the men could party with. They send a dozen and those women can give as good as they get so you're off the hook for tonight because the guys will have zero interest in sex. So we have a barbecue a few drinks and call it a night."

"Great just what I was hoping for. To be honest my heart isn't into a raunchy night of sex with anyone other than you, Garrett and Logan."

"Done, now what are you doing after your milking?"

"I'm going for a walk get some fresh air, as nice as this house is one needs some outdoor time too."

"How's the wolf project going?"

"Fine, all the paperwork is done and submitted, now I wait for their answer and voila by next spring at the latest we have transplants in Montana."

"Well great, now we should do your milking you seem full."

"Ok, lets get it done."

Dillon led the way into the sunroom now referred to as the milking room Garrett bringing up the rear of the threesome.

"Where is Logan this morning?" Amiela asked nonchalantly.

"He had some errands to run, said something about a package he had to pick up in the city."

Garrett helped her off with her robe while Dillon sorted the equipment.

Sitting on the milking bench taking in the view she never seem to tire of while Dillon hooked her up to the breast cups. Garrett stepped behind her massaging her shoulders relaxing her body so her milk would let down more easily.

Dillon turned the machine on and she felt the dildo split her open as it pumped in ever deepening strokes. Her milk streamed down the tubes then started to gush as her first orgasm of the day commenced. A second bloomed before she could catch her breath from the first and the whole time Garrett stood behind her massaging her arms shoulders and upper chest.

After her sixth orgasm in quick succession her breasts had expelled all the milk they were going to. Dillon shut the machine off and unhooked her, Garrett helped her stand holding her robe so she could slip her arms into it.

Catching her breath she said 'I'm going for a shower and then I think  I will go for that walk." Leaving the two men behind as she made her way to the suite she now looked on as her sanctuary. No one bothered her here Dillon and Logan slept with her sometimes and others it was just one or neither of them, so more and more she looked at this space as hers.

Starting the shower she hadn't heard the knock on the door only her name spoken from Garrett's

lips. "Amiela do you want me to take the cuffs off?"

"I'd forgotten all about them to be honest, but yes I expect showering will be much easier without them." Garrett produced a key unlocking her wrists first then her ankles putting them in her dressing room in the handcrafted box they came in. Putting the key in the depression provided beside the other keys.

"Ok you're all set, I can't remove the necklace Dillon ordered it to stay on and no the key for your cuffs does not work on it."

"Well shit I don't know what he is expecting this to do, but whatever it is its a big fat failure."

"Its ok Amiela he'll remove it shortly once he sees things aren't going his way."

"I hope you're right, I like wearing jewellery and everything but I also like to remove it when I like to go bare. The body rings aside I love them and it seems he wants something to do with removing and replacing them so be it, but everything else I choose."

Garrett stepped in close putting his arms around her hugging her and immediately she felt better.

"Good now?"

"Yes, you gave me just what I needed." He stepped back drawing her to the bed tucking her between his knees.

"You know Amiela living and loving dominants is always going to be a give and take situation for you, mostly give on your part. Accept this of them or walk away because if you can't that one thing will make all your lives miserable."

"I know, and I do accept that, I even understand it my father's are very much the same way but sometimes I would like to say no and see what happens aside from an all out screaming match. Take this necklace for example I should be able to take it off if I want."

"Ok well explain this to them and see what happens. Have you told either of them that you are losing weight?"

"No I haven't mentioned it and they haven't noticed. Its not a big concern at least not yet."

"You are thin enough, a few more weeks and it will be dangerous for you. Tell them or I will."

"I promise today as soon as I can get both of them alone."

Garrett was pacified by her declaration so let it be.

"I'm going so I will see you later." Giving her a peck on the cheek he left leaving her with fluttering feeling in the pit of her stomach. She rushed through her shower brushed out her wet hair and piled it on her head clipping it in place. Brushing her teeth she thought about what to wear shorts and a light blouse would do it. Her athletic walking shoes as she planned a long trek.

Dressed she gathered a hat and her sunglasses leaving the suite she walked down the hall stopping at the head of the stairs she looked down and saw Garrett waiting at the bottom.

Walking down the stairs she wondered what he was up to, a smile formed on her lips matching his. Meeting him at the bottom solved the mystery.

"I thought I would join you if that's ok? Figured I could use some fresh air since I've been cooped up for a couple of days."

"Sure that's alright.

They set off out the front door heading south toward the barns and the outbuildings and the open prairie beyond. By the side of the garage they used for equipment repairs and such Amiela's fifth wheel sat undisturbed with her truck sitting just in front of it but not hooked up.

"What's the fifth wheel about? I didn't think Dillon and Logan were much into camping."

"Their not, its mine, I use it in the field when I study a pack for an extended period of time."

"May I see inside?"

"Into camping are you?"

"As a matter of fact I have a rig at home I use to go fishing and hunting sometimes."

"Sure why not, its thirty five feet, large shower, king size bed and a kitchen and living room I adore."

Unlocking the door she went up the steps disappearing inside Garrett followed making sure no one was watching."

Garrett took in all the details of the RV approving of all the luxury touches the rig offered, a very comfortable home away from home. When he went up the two steps to the bedroom he was amazed to find wolves, stuffed toy wolf animals lined up on the dresser. Bouncing on the king size bed he approved again. The bed would be so lovely like sleeping on a cloud.

"Garrett are you alright?" Amiela asked stepping into the bedroom.

"I'm fine, great in fact, where did you find this bed I want one, hell I want a lot for every bedroom."

He was smiling and so exuberant she found it infectious and started to giggle uncontrollably. Grabbing her arm he pulled her down on the bed and kissed her till she was squirming and hot beneath him. Breaking the kiss she gasped out "You either have to stop or fuck me right here and now."

Stroking the side of her face he replied with a smile on his lips.

"I would like nothing more than to make love to you, but I find myself without any condoms so this will have to wait till later. Shall we continue our walk?"

Amiela was a little disappointed consoling herself there would be time later.

"Sure let's go before our common sense eludes us again."

Leaving the RV they walked out past the barns which were quiet as all the horses were out to pasture and all the hands were out checking on them. Any wolf activity around the herds were reported directly to her so she could track and account the wolf pack's territory and movements.

The prairie stretched before them with the mountains standing sentry over it all, the spring flowers were coming to an end as summer approached giving way to new blooms dotting the vast expanse of land the McLean's called home.

"Do you have these views at your place?"

"Sure do only the mountains are a bit closer. You'll have to come and see for yourself, you will love it!"

His exuberance was so infectious she found herself joining him in his joy. Taking his hand in hers they walked till they found a rocky outcrop where they discovered a spring bubbling merrily over the rocks into a saddle shaped pool.

"This is called saddle spring." Garrett told her mentioning that some hundred years ago one of the Mclean ancestors had lost his saddle in this very spot when his cinch broke.

They sat for awhile just listening to the water tinkle over the rocks and slide into the pool enjoying their shared silence.

"So that is why it's called saddle spring?"

"Yep no point in thinking to come up with something when its right there in front of you, besides they had more important things to do than think up names. Do you know that Dillon and Logan are the first in four generations to be involved in a tri relationship?"

"No I didn't, I'm like the sixteenth generation or something like that to be involved in one. How about your family any multiple pairings?"

"There is yes but ours tend to be more of the quad variety. My mother was married to three brothers, and back through time with the odd couple or tri but the majority are quads."

Looking Garrett over she realized she had questions she didn't know why it mattered so much to her but it did.

"I just realized I don't even know your last name, what is it?"

"Mason and yours I know, I did a online search and came up with some pretty impressive facts about you."

"The awards accolades and all the rest is just fodder for universities and donors, it doesn't really mean a whole lot to me. Getting out in the field researching studying that's what really impresses me."

"You know for a dominant you're not that way all the time."

"No my dominance shows when I strap a woman to a horse or other such device, then I'm the master and in my work but otherwise you get easy going me."

"I like this me most of all."

"I like this you too, but I do have a softness for the submissive you as well."

This made Amiela blush scarlet which Garrett found very sexy."

"Shall we head back its almost lunch, Dillon said Logan would be back by then. Perfect time for you to mention your weight loss."

"Ok let's go I'm getting hungry anyway."

Arriving at the house at half past the lunch hour they strolled into the kitchen hand in hand finding Logan and Dillon with burgers and a green salad already and waiting on the table.

"Hey you two, I hoped you would be back in time for lunch." Dillon stated with a smile and a questioning look in his eyes he directed to Garrett which he ignored choosing not to comment.

Logan came out of the bathroom looking expectantly from Amiela to Garrett and back.

They took turns washing up in the bathroom then sat at the table for lunch helping themselves to everything. Logan poured red wine to go with the meal then sat back enjoying the conversation buzzing around him.

With a nudge of Garrett's knee against hers she found words to explain one of the issues pressing on her mind.

"I'm glad to have you all alone because I'm losing weight about two pounds a week and no matter what or how much I eat I cannot maintain it. I just keep losing, so perhaps you may find a solution to this before it becomes serious." There she said it had been thinking of telling them for a couple of weeks, just couldn't find the words or the courage.

Logan and Dillon sat stunned by her declaration it was Dillon who finally spoke.

"Ok well your hormone dosage will have to be lowered which may or may not reduce the quantity of milk you're producing. Your next dose is suspended and we'll go with one a day instead of two.
In the morning I will weigh you and every morning till we see if that does it or not. If we need to we can always take other steps to solve the problem."

Garrett massaged her leg under the table as if he was saying see that wasn't so bad now was it. Giving him a sideways look confirmed it for her.

Logan drank his wine then set his glass down, taking in both Amiela and Garrett with an expectant look on his face.

"Garrett Dillon and I would like you to join us in taking care and sharing Amiela. Would you be agreeable to the proposition?"

Garrett took a drink from his glass and began "Only if Amiela agrees to it, and I do expect her and I to get better acquainted and fall in love if that's in the offing for us." He had been thinking about this very thing not an hour ago as they walked back to the house, now here it was.

All eyes turned to her making her nervous and unsure of herself. "Are you in agreement with the proposal Amiela?" Logan asked the dominant coming through loud and clear. She knew he would just prefer to tell her how things would be, much simpler in his mind.

"Yes I agree, I think a foursome rounds things out nicely. You all complement each other and me."

"Ok then a celebration is in order tonight we have the guests but tomorrow night it will just be us so how about we do both make it a two day event?" Logan asked merriment in his eyes.

After each agreed he continued. "We will all work out schedules and time with Amiela. Your suite will be only yours to do with as you please. Dillon and I will move into the rooms we used before you came, truth be told we never really moved out. Garrett can have the suite he now occupies when he's here. We will try to give you equal time with each of us, the other details we'll negotiate then put in legal jargon our lawyer, and yours will draw up the agreement, all agreed."

They agreed with a clinking of glasses looking forward to their new found arrangement.

Excusing herself Amiela went up to her suite to mash through all that had happened in the last few days. She had agreed to a foursome of which Garrett was one, she liked him alot and given a little time she could see herself falling in love with him as deeply as she loved Dillon and Logan. She had searched a long long time to get into a relationship to her liking now it was perfect, she had three terrific men who would do anything for her. She had almost everything she had always wanted and children would come.

A knock on the door brought her out of her thoughts, she went and opened it finding Garrett on the other side with a bottle of wine and two glasses.

"I want to talk to you?" Dominant Garrett was back.

"Come on in, have a seat."

Settling on the sofa facing each other he poured the wine then dove in.

"That was quite a surprise from Dillon and Logan to invite me to share you. Do you really want this?"

"Yes, I do. Its like I said we compliment each other in all the right ways. This should work wonderfully well."

"What about children, do you want them?"

"Yes absolutely in a couple of years, my wolves take precedence till then."

"Ok, why do you have all those wolf animal toys in your RV?" His smile was wide and infectious.

"Each one is a wolf I have transplanted to a new area for repopulation. Those are my awards and rewards."

"I didn't find anything about that in the internet search I did."

"Ok smartass, its just my way."

" I find it and you adorable. I don't know how I ending up getting you but I'm very happy I have. Now I don't have to settle for tidbits of you I have all of you."

"As do Logan and Dillon, speaking of which where are they?"

"Entertaining the guests and looking forward to their departure."

"In the interest of getting to know each other what do you do for a career besides ranching?"

"I'm an engineer, my specialty is reconstruction projects and I also do research mostly to do with female hormones etc."

"Hmm that all sounds interesting but why so many degrees?"

"My parents figured if one was good many was much better."

"I understand completely, my parents are very much the same way although they were more than pleased when I finished my degree and went off in search of wolves, although lately I've been getting the impression they want more from me. I guess that explains the setup with Dillon and Logan, they will have an absolute cow when I tell them about you."

"Meaning what exactly?"

"It is something I don't think they bargained for three son in laws as opposed to two."

"So you're thinking of marriage and not just living together."

"As traditional as that concept is yes."

"Good cause so am I. So the agenda for tonight is we go down anytime before the barbecue starts so we should get you changed."

"You're picking my clothes this evening?"

"Yes, and it won't be anything like Dillon and Logan chose for you. I'm going a bit tamer."

Amiela got in and out of the shower in quick order to find Garrett going through her closet piece by piece trying to find the perfect outfit, he picked a mid thigh halter dress with a plunging neckline that would come to the the bottom of her cleavage. Ok a little tamer she thought at least my ass will be covered and all the other bits she would rather have covered.

"I do love seeing you in the tiny dresses too, but since this is about a nice relaxed evening with no sex at least with the guests I thought something a little more conservative. "

Turning it back to front on the hanger she was impressed with the black and shimmering gold flower design,with an open back. The sandals he held in his other hand black three inch heels with gold buckles. Presentable with the necklace she was still wearing.

"What about earrings Garrett?"

"A gold hoop medium size, here I will go choose them for you. Get dressed."

What he came back with was a gold hoop but they also had black, white and blue diamonds dangling from them.

"Good choice now everything will flow nicely."

Surveying herself in the mirror she liked what she presented, leaving her hair loose worked well, just the right amount of mystery.

"What do you think?"

"Stunning, shall we go?"

Leaving the suite they walked down the hall hearing silence, milking time was coming around and she wondered how that would be handled tonight, this morning was awesome just Dillon and Garrett perhaps they would do that again.

They descended the stairs looking down seeing no one, at the bottom they proceeded to the great room and the patio beyond. All the play equipment was gone just the usual furnishings remained.

Amiela was relieved she could enjoy herself and not worry about who wanted to fuck her in front of who.

Breezing through the doors on Garrett's arm he seated her at an empty table then went to get her a drink. Returning with her wine he seated himself beside the most desirable woman he had ever met. It was comfortable and natural for them to be together, he couldn't wait to make everything official.

Men crowded around the table thanking Amiela for her hospitality, they all said they would be back if they received another invite.

She wanted to have the time to get acquainted with Garrett maybe even go fishing with him for a few days.

"You seem a million miles away. Care to share?"

"I was just thinking about going fishing with you and seeing your ranch."

"That can be arranged on our week together, Logan thinks a week with each of us is good to start. Now if you travel with me them we may do a bit longer with each of the others getting equal time. This is going to work out just fine."

"I think so too, one thing my mom always said, is it not easy living with three men but I think this might be a bit easier because you all have different careers and interests. So you won't get in each others way at least when it comes to me."

"True, we should slip away and get your milking done before dinner."

"Yes, that would be great I'm getting a little uncomfortable."

Finishing their wine, both rose heading through the great room to the kitchen and the sun/milking room beyond.

Logan noticed they had left and knew why, Garrett was in charge of milking her tonight. Getting everyone's attention he announced "Amiela is about to be milked would anyone care to watch the proceedings?"

A round of yes's could be heard around the room. Picking up the remote from the fireplace mantle her switched the large screen TV on. There she was bent over her hands on the arm of a chair her breasts encased in the milkers and Garrett behind her already inside pumping away if the look on her face was anything to go by, pure lust and carnal need radiated out from her a tangible feeling felt throughout the room.

Milk filled the tubes frothing into the collection bottles as Amiela came and then again. The orgasms continued, her milk flowed with Garrett fucking her at a furious pace trying to reach his own peak. Slowing the pace he eased her through a tremendous orgasm giving her time to catch her breath after she stopped moaning and screaming.

Looking around Logan saw evidence on all the men's faces wishing they were the one to be milking her tonight.

Watching the screen they saw Amiela come in and out of yet another orgasm as Garrett produced his own. The milk gushed down the tubes then dwindled to a small stream, a few seconds later it quit entirely. Logan figured she had given her normal amount for today, tomorrow he expected to see less as her hormones levelled out a little.

He switched the TV off as Amiela pulled the dress over her head, she and Garrett had showered afterward giving everyone in the room a glimpse of how truly suited they were teasing and fondling each other as they washed.

Garrett and Amiela reappeared at the party none the wiser to the viewing the guests had been treated to, curious and some lustful stares followed them to their table, oblivious to all this as they only had eyes and hands for each other.

Logan was pleased with the way matters had progressed as his and Dillon's need to watch would be filled with Garrett around now.

Food and beverages flowed the party reached its peak, as guests went off to find their beds Garrett decided it was time for he and Amiela to do the same.

Making their way up the stairs to Amiela's suite they stopped a question forming in her eyes.

"Aren't we going to your room?"

"No, I thought you may like some time on your own."

"No I want to be with you, I want you to make love to me. Could you find the enthusiasm to fulfill that wish for me?"

Touching her nose with his index finger then kissing her till her toes curled inside her shoes he replied with a devilish gleam in his eyes.

"Your wish is granted, yours or mine?"

"Well we're right here with a lovely gigantic bed just inside, so I think mine."

Entering the suite Garrett was peeling her dress off before the door closed, kneeling at her feet he removed her shoes then proceeded to delve his tongue inside her baby soft pussy. She opened her legs wide to allow him all the access he desired. Walking her backward till she fell back onto the bed with a omph. Releasing her long enough to gather her up placing her squarely on the bed he resumed his assault on her feminine core eliciting scream,whimpers and moans of satisfaction as her orgasm took her.

Hopping off the bed he disrobed in record time joining her on the bed, parting her legs wide he thrust into the hilt letting out a groan at how tight she still was even after they had each other not but a few hours before. Lightheaded with all the blood pumping into his penis he thrust hard and fast cuming as she did. Rolling to his side taking her with him still lodged within her tight channel he stroked her back as their breathing normalized.

Picking the quilt off the end of the bed he covered them, after several minutes in the snuggly warmth they drifted off each to their dreams.

Waking later than normal the sun had trekked beyond the east windows telling Garrett it was around ten o'clock, looking over Amiela was curled on her side where he left her. His arm had fallen asleep under her head but that was alright, he kissed her awake removing his arm when she moved to turn over and face him. Flexing his fingers to restore circulation he kept kissing her until she tried to speak.

"I need to be milked, I'm starting to leak."

Placing his hand on her breast he found a drop of moisture. Getting up he retrieved a robe helping her into it then threw on his jeans and shirt.

"Ok lets go and get you milked."

Leaving the suite they made their way down to the sunroom without seeing a single soul, stripping her robe off Garrett strapped the milking harness onto her sat her on the stool and turned the milker on. The dildo split her open pumping away mimicking a real cock. Within minutes she orgasmed and milked flowed fast into the collection bottles.

Garrett watched her for twenty minutes until the flow had lessened then went into the kitchen made coffee and poured orange juice for himself and Amiela.

Figuring she would be done, he went and unhooked her and helped her back into her robe.

Telling her there was coffee and juice in the kitchen he cleaned the equipment, put the milk in the refrigerator and went out to see her.

Walking into the kitchen he found Dillon at the stove making pancakes and sausage, Logan was sitting beside Amiela at the table laughing over something she said. Everyone seemed very happy which made his mood even brighter.

"Good morning guys, did all the guests leave?"

"Yes this morning, the last one took the helicopter at eight. Now its time for us to celebrate." Logan replied relaxed and content.

Dillon brought the food over to the table while Garrett grabbed a coffee and more juice.

"What's the plan for this celebration?" Garrett asked wondering.

"In due time my friend, for now we just eat relax and enjoy."

Halfway through breakfast the doorbell chimed taking Logan off to answer it, no one else paid it much attention just continued eating until their plates were empty and their stomachs were satisfied.

"How do you feel Amiela?" Dillon asked giving no hint to where he was heading with the question.

"Fine, not so drained as before. I have more energy and my sex drive has lessened to tolerable levels. Mind you I still want to have sex at least a couple of times a day sometimes more."

"Good we'll give it a week and see if your weight stabilizes, where is your weight at?"

"One hundred pounds as of day before yesterday."

"And your usual was what 120."

"Yes, I've maintained that weight for years."

Just then Logan reappeared noticing everyone was finished, he had a secretive look on his face.

"Join me in the living room everyone. There's something I want to show you all."

Stepping into the living room after Logan with Dillon and Garrett following she was amazed to find the entire room filled flowers all her favorites roses of almost every colour, carnations, lilies, and even mums and a few pots of herbs.

"What did you do Logan buy out the whole flower shop?"

"Yeh pretty much, I wanted you to have all your favorites."

Taking her by the hand he seated her on the sofa kneeling on one knee he asked "Amiela will you marry me?" Followed by the same declaration from Dillon and Garrett.

She was stunned, no matter how many times she had the vision of it being exactly like this she was at a loss for words. Swallowing then finding her voice.

"Yes I will marry you Logan, Dillon and Garrett."

Logan produced three rings handing one to Dillon and one to Garrett, he held the black diamond band slipping it onto her ring finger then stood moving aside while Dillon slipped a sapphire band on her finger and Garrett slipped a white diamond band onto her finger making it official they were engaged. She noticed the bands fit together in a very intricate pattern much like the four of them. Seating themselves around her Dillon explained how things would work.

"You will marry all of us in a private ceremony only family and close friends who embrace the lifestyle. But you will have to choose one of us to marry legally."

"I will marry all three of you in our ceremony but I will not choose one to marry legally. I will be married to all of you in every sense of the word marriage."

Satisfied with her answer they all knew they could make the necessary legal arrangements to satisfy any issues.

Logan cleared his throat saying. "One more thing for you." He handed her a sealed envelope  which she opened and read.

Stocks worth 10.2 million set in trust for wolf research was the gist of it.

"How did this happen?" She asked shocked.

"We sold your milk and invested the profits over the last several months and here you are enough money to do as you wish on any wolf research you wish all privately funded thanks to your high demand milk."

Dillon slipped away finding champagne and glasses returning he opened the bottle poured the white sparkling liquid into the glasses handing them around he said.

"To us."

Everyone agreed, excited about the new life they were embarking on.

www.ingramcontent.com/pod-product-compliance
Lightning Source LLC
Chambersburg PA
CBHW070332130626
46556CB00007B/2832